Palmetto Island

Muddy Bottom

ASHLEY FARLEY

ALSO BY ASHLEY FARLEY

Hope Springs Series

Dream Big, Stella!

Show Me the Way

Mistletoe and Wedding Bells

Stand Alone

Tangled in Ivy

Lies that Bind

Life on Loan

Only One Life

Home for Wounded Hearts

Nell and Lady

Sweet Tea Tuesdays

Saving Ben

Sweeney Sisters Series

Saturdays at Sweeney's

Tangle of Strings

Boots and Bedlam

Lowcountry Stranger

Her Sister's Shoes

Magnolia Series

Beyond the Garden

Magnolia Nights

Scottie's Adventures

Breaking the Story

Merry Mary

ONE

From her kitchen window, Birdie watches the sun rise over the inlet. Pink sky atop golden marsh and murky water. A new day. A new year. A fresh start. Aside from a gust of wind rippling the water, the inlet is quiet, the world sleeping off last night's celebration.

What does this year hold for her? Will she expand her pie business? Or will this be the year she returns to nursing? Baking satisfies a creative side she's only recently discovered and keeps her connected to friends and acquaintances she wouldn't otherwise see. Watching her business flourish has become one of the few joys in an otherwise mundane life. Humdrum, her mama used to call it. Isn't that the norm for middle age?

Casting frequent glances at the window, Birdie rolls out her first batch of pie crusts. Rum is the pie flavor of month. Her grandmother's recipe is the best she's ever tasted, but the directions are complicated, and by the time she places three pies in the oven, it's going on nine o'clock. She's surprised and slightly concerned her husband hasn't returned home from kayaking. Cary rarely misses an opportunity to sleep in, especially on holidays. But they'd gone to bed early, choosing not to usher in the

New Year, and he was gone when she woke a few minutes before dawn.

Retrieving her fleece from the coat closet, she slips out the back door, crosses the screen porch, and makes her way down the path to the creek. On the other side of the wooden storage shed that houses life preservers and fishing equipment, she discovers Cary's kayak in the bottom slot of the log rack. Turning away from the rack, she sees their center console boat tied to the dock and, up at the house, Cary's car in the driveway alongside Birdie's and their daughter's.

Where could her husband possibly be at such an early hour on New Year's Day?

Wrapping her fleece tighter, she hurries up to the attached garage where she finds Cary's bicycle hanging from a rack alongside his hunting waders. Birdie enters the house through the kitchen and darts up the stairs to their bedroom. His wallet is on top of their chest of drawers, his iPad and iPhone charging on his bedside table. In their shared walk-in closet, his suits and starched dress shirts hang according to color in a neat row. His carry-on suitcase, the only one he owns, is parked beneath the built-in shelves that house his shoes.

Heart pounding in ears, Birdie scours the house from attic to utility basement, checking in closets and under beds. Cary is nowhere in sight. *Wait!* There's one room left to search. Why didn't she think of it sooner? Cary must be with Hannah. When their daughter was a child, Cary read to her nearly every night. During Hannah's teenage years, Birdie often found him sitting in the rocker beside her bed late at night, watching Hannah sleep. He must have gone into her room to kiss her goodnight and nodded off in the rocker.

She takes the stairs two at a time on the way back to the second floor. Cracking Hannah's door open, she peeks inside. Her daughter is sleeping in a ball on her side, palms pressed together and wedged between cheek and pillow. The rocker beside her bed is empty.

Hannah sits bolt upright, her eyes darting about the room as she gets her bearings. She falls back against the pillow and closes her eyes. She's relieved to be freed from her dream—the one where she's preparing to take a final exam, but she hasn't been to a single class all semester. Hannah is a diligent student. She would never allow that to happen. With only twelve hours remaining for the upcoming spring semester, she's on track to graduate summa cum laude in May.

Her mother shakes her. "Hannah! Wake up!" Birdie's tone is urgent, her grip on Hannah's arm tight. "Did your dad say anything about going hunting or fishing this morning?"

Hannah swings her feet off the side of the bed. "What? No. Why?"

"He's missing. The boat and all the kayaks are here. So is his car, bicycle, wallet, and iPhone."

Hannah rubs the sleep from her eyes. "What about his clothes?"

Birdie paces back and forth, making Hannah dizzy. "His suitcase is in his closet, but considering all the clothes he owns, I wouldn't know if anything is missing."

Hannah stands, hooking her arm around the bedpost until the lightheadedness passes. "This is crazy, Mom. Dad didn't just vanish. He's a grown man. It's not like someone kidnapped him. He probably went fishing with one of his friends. I'm sure he'll be back soon."

"I didn't think of that, but it makes sense. Whoever he went fishing with picked him up. Still, I think it's strange he didn't mention it last night."

"I need coffee." Hannah brushes past her mother, who follows her down the hall and stairs to the kitchen.

Hannah pops a pod into the coffeemaker, and as she stares at the steaming brew stream into her mug, she's struck by a memory of a conversation she had with her dad on her first night home from college two weeks ago. Closer to her father than her mother, she's always gone to him with all her problems. She expected him to be furious when she delivered the news. Instead, his eyes had filled with tears.

"Let's not spoil Christmas," he'd said. "We'll wait until after New Year's to tell your mother."

At the time, she didn't think much of the remorseful tone in his voice. But now, she can't help but wonder. Was he planning to leave them? Did he know he wouldn't be here after New Year's? Was he buying himself time, so he wouldn't have to deal with Hannah's problem?

Her mother returns to baking while Hannah moves from window to window, watching for a car in the driveway or a boat at the dock. Every moment that ticks off the clock on the mantel in the family room makes the situation more of a reality. Her father didn't go fishing, and he isn't coming home. Not today. Maybe never.

After an hour, she returns to the kitchen where Birdie is preparing the filling for pecan pies. "We should call someone."

Her mom looks up from the mixing bowl. "Call someone about what?"

"About Dad, Mom. Duh."

"Oh. That." Birdie brushes a strand of yellow hair off her face, leaving a smudge of flour on her cheek. "I overreacted earlier. I'm sure you're right. He's off fishing with one of his friends. He'll be home soon."

Hannah grips the edge of the granite countertop. "I'm not so sure anymore."

Her mother's body goes still. "What makes you say that?"

"I remembered a conversation I had with Dad before Christmas. Something was off about it . . . about him. At least call his friends' wives?"

"And say what to them at ten thirty in the morning on New Year's Day? I lost my husband. Is he by any chance with yours?"

Hannah sees her mother's point. Word of her missing father would spread through their small community like a slab of butter melting over hot grits. What if he didn't leave them? What if . . . The scenario that pops into Hannah's head is too devastating to consider. "Then call Chief Summers. He'll know what to do."

Birdie abandons her spatula in her mixing bowl. "It's way too early to get the police involved. We'll look like fools when your father shows up with a cooler full of trout."

"What if he isn't fishing? What if something bad happened to him? What if he got up during the night to pee, fell and hit his head, and now he's wandering around the island with amnesia?" Having no desire to deal with a hysterical Birdie, Hannah decides to leave out her most serious concerns. "We're wasting time. The chief is your best friend's nephew."

"Exactly why I don't want to call him. I'm not ready to talk about this with Max."

"Why would the chief tell Max? I'm sure he's bound by the law to keep situations like these confidential. If nothing else, he'll tell us whether we should be alarmed."

"Maybe you're right," Birdie says, removing her cell phone from her apron pocket. "I'll give Toby a call."

Hannah learns little from her mother's side of the conversation, and the minute Birdie hangs up with the chief, she says, "Well?"

"Toby doubts your father would've gone fishing. Nothing has been biting lately. But he wants me to call his friends, anyway. There's always the possibility he went hunting, even though his waders are in the garage."

Birdie sits down at the table in the adjoining breakfast room, and Hannah brews two cups of green tea before joining her. Birdie calls Eleanor, Cecilia, and Ellen, but Perry, Gerald, and Brendan know nothing of her father's whereabouts. Ellen presses her mom for more information, and Birdie, a terrible liar, confesses, "He was gone when I woke up. Everything he owns—his car and wallet and phone—is still here."

Birdie slams her phone down on the table. "Stupid me. The entire town will know your father is missing within the hour."

"Let them gossip. I'm more concerned about Dad." She nods at her mother's phone on the table. "Call Chief Summers back. Tell him no one has seen Dad."

Toby promises to alert his officers of Cary's disappearance. "We'll be on the lookout," he says. "I'll make some calls and be back in touch. In the meantime, let me know immediately if you hear from him."

Hannah and Birdie remain at the kitchen table, waiting and watching and drinking cup after cup of herbal tea. When lunchtime rolls around, Birdie heats up leftover chili, but their bowls remain untouched on the table in front of them.

Around two o'clock, when the first of Birdie's customers comes to claim her pie, Hannah turns her away. "Sorry. No pies today. Mom isn't feeling well."

"Put a sign on the door," Birdie demands. "Tell them I'm sick."

Hannah scrawls the note with a black marker on computer paper and duct-tapes it to the front door. She's no sooner returned to the table when Toby calls.

"I've checked the local train and bus stations and the airport in Charleston. There's no sign of him, unless he's traveling under an assumed name. I'm calling in the Coast Guard."

Birdie bites down on a balled fist to stifle a sob.

"I know this is hard, Birdie, but I have to ask. Is there any reason Cary might have tried to hurt himself?"

"You mean . . . like . . ." Hannah casts a nervous glance at her daughter.

Toby finishes her sentence. "Suicide. I can't ignore the possibility." He breathes heavily into the phone. "If Cary didn't take his phone or wallet . . . considering your proximity to the inlet—"

"Do what you think best," Birdie snaps and ends the call.

Hannah and Birdie sit in silence, acutely aware of the helicopters flying overhead and the diesel engines rumbling on the boats searching the waters near their property. The landline rings multiple times with calls from nosy neighbors, but they don't answer the phone. And when dusk falls over the room, they don't bother turning on any lights.

Around seven o'clock, Birdie breaks the silence. "Why don't you tell me about your conversation with your dad before Christmas? What was off about it?"

Hannah looks up, but she doesn't meet Birdie's gaze. "We don't need to get into that now."

"I disagree. If there's any chance it had something to do with his disappearance, I should know about it."

Hannah pushes back from the table, kicking her chair out of the way as she stands. "Dad didn't leave because of me, Mom. You're his wife. If he abandoned us, it's because of you." Turning her back on Birdie, Hannah moves over to the window.

Birdie goes to stand beside her daughter. "I'm grasping at straws, Hannah. If you know something that might help us find him, you need to tell me."

"I don't think Dad wants to be found," Hannah mumbles. Strobe lights from the rescue boat flash across her daughter's lovely face, illuminating her olive-green eyes. "I shared some news with him. He said let's not spoil Christmas, and he wanted me to wait until after New Year's to tell you. It makes

7

sense, now. He knew he'd be gone and wouldn't have to deal with it."

Fear crawls down Birdie's spine. "Deal with what, sweetheart?"

"My pregnancy," Hannah says, her words barely audible.

"Your what?"

"You heard me, Mom. I'm pregnant."

Anger pulses through Birdie. "How did this happen?"

"The usual way," Hannah says, her gaze steady on the Coast Guard boat.

"Don't get smart with me, young lady." Crossing the room to the pine hutch, she pours a shot of vodka, swallows it, and refills the shot glass. Pointing the glass at Hannah, she says, "I've talked to you time and again about practicing safe sex. Did you stop taking the pill?"

"I went away for the weekend with some friends, and I forgot to take my packet of pills with me. I didn't think missing two pills would matter. Apparently, it does. I'm sorry. I got careless."

"You're *sorry*? You've just ruined your life, and all you can say is you're *sorry*?" Birdie kicks back the vodka and slams down the glass. "Who's the father?"

Hannah's shoulders slump. "I'm not sure. I hooked up with a couple of different guys that weekend."

Birdie is grateful for the distance between them. She's never been this mad at her child before. "Great, Hannah. Just great. How far along are you? Have you seen a doctor?"

Lowering her head, Hannah stares at the floor. "I went to see Dr. Pendleton last week. I'm almost nine weeks."

"Good. You still have time to take care of it."

Hannah's head jerks up. "Are you suggesting I have an abortion?"

Birdie blinks hard. "Yes! That's exactly what I'm suggesting. You're not seriously considering raising a bastard child on your own, are you?"

Hannah places her hand on her stomach. "Whether or not you approve, I'm keeping this baby."

Birdie grips the neck of the Grey Goose bottle. "I've had enough of this day." Spinning on her heels, she dashes up the stairs to her room.

TWO

Birdie cracks the seal on a new Grey Goose bottle and adds a splash of vodka to her coffee. She needs something stronger than Advil to cure this headache. Her husband is missing. Her daughter is pregnant. Her peaceful life is over. She's entitled to drown her sorrows.

Mug in hand, she stands at the kitchen window. Heavy fog blankets the inlet, preventing the Coast Guard from continuing their search. How late did they stay out last night? She remembers little after hearing the report of a missing man on the local news at eleven.

Her phone rings on the kitchen island with a call from Toby. She snatches up the phone. "Did you find anything?"

"No. And we're not going to. I'm sorry, Birdie, but we're calling off the search. Based on my investigation, I have reason to believe Cary left town on his own volition."

Birdie's stomach clenches, and she thinks she might throw up. "What reason? What're you talking about?"

"I just got off the phone with Jonathan Hart. He can explain better than me. He'll be calling you momentarily." Toby lets out an audible sigh. "I'm so sorry, Birdie. Let me know if I can help in any other way."

"Wait—"

The line goes dead.

She stumbles to the nearest chair, sets her phone, screen-up, on the table, and waits for Cary's law partner to call. Her nerves are frazzled. She can't take more bad news. But she has a sick feeling Jonathan is about to tell her the worst yet.

Fifteen minutes later, the back door swings open, and Jonathan enters in a rush of frigid air. "This is serious business, Birdie. I figured I'd better tell you in person." He pulls her to her feet and hugs her tight. "I'm so sorry. I can't believe Cary didn't tell you. If I had known, I would've told you myself."

Birdie pushes her old friend away. "Told me what, Jonathan? What on earth is going on?"

"Let's sit down." He moves a chair close to hers, and they sit with knees touching. "We forced Cary to resign from the firm a month ago, right after Thanksgiving. He was . . . um . . . mismanaging our funds."

Birdie's blue eyes narrow. "Mismanaging, as in embezzling?"

Jonathan gives his head a solemn nod.

"We've been friends forever, Jonathan. Couldn't you have given him a second chance?"

Jonathan hangs his head. "That *was* the second chance. Since then, we've hired a forensic accountant who has uncovered even more theft. Amounts we can't overlook. I spoke with Cary a few days ago. I warned him we will be pressing charges."

Planting her elbows on the table, Birdie buries her face in her hands. "This keeps getting worse and worse."

"And there's still more. Cary has been spotted around town with another woman."

Birdie peeks at him through her fingers. "Spotted by whom?"

"Me. And some guys at the office. And my wife."

Birdie lowers her hands from her face. "Who is this woman?"

"No one seems to know."

"Cary's electronic devices are here," Birdie says. "If he's been corresponding with her via email or text messages, the police can identify the woman."

"Cary's too smart for that. If those devices have any incriminating evidence on them, he wouldn't have left them behind. He undoubtedly purchased a new phone to communicate with her. This woman, whoever she is, helped him execute his disappearance. They deserve each other. And you deserve better." Jonathan places his hand on Birdie's forearm. "This may be hard for you to believe now, but I've known Cary all my life, and one day, you'll understand how much better off you are without him."

On her way to the kitchen, Hannah stops short at the sound of her uncle's voice. Jonathan isn't really her uncle. He's her godfather. He's also her father's law partner and best childhood friend. Pressed against the wall outside the kitchen, she eavesdrops on his conversation with her mother. She can't believe her ears. Her father stole money from his law firm, and they're going to press charges. The other woman part comes as a shock, but not as much as it would've twenty-four hours ago.

Hannah hears chairs dragging across the floor, followed by murmured voices as her mother sees Jonathan out. The back door clicks shut, and when her mom storms past, Hannah steps in line behind her, following her through the family room to the small home office her parents share.

Sitting down at the desk, Birdie types on the keyboard as she accesses their online banking accounts. She touches her fingertip to the screen and scrutinizes the digital statements. "That bastard. I should never have allowed him to handle our household expenses. He cleaned out our accounts."

"How much was in each?" Hannah asks, peering over her shoulder.

"I'm not concerned about the checking account. That balance fluctuates. But the last time I checked the money market and brokerage accounts,"—Birdie's gaze lifts upward as though looking for the answer on the ceiling—"sometime around the beginning of December, we had fifty thousand in our money market and our brokerage account was worth a half-million dollars."

Hannah's jaw drops. "What? That's an insane amount of money."

"It's a lot of money. It's your father's life savings." Birdie pounds the desk with her fist. "Damn him!"

Hannah summons the courage to ask, "Will we have to sell the house?"

"I don't know, honey. We've owned this house for twenty years. We no longer have a mortgage. But I have no idea how much utilities and maintenance expenses run. Your father handled all that."

Hannah sits on the edge of the desk. "I don't understand, Mom. Why was Dad managing the firm's finances in the first place?"

Birdie falls back in her chair. "Your father graduated from college with a degree in accounting. He got his CPA license before deciding to go to law school. By managing the firm's accounts, Cary saved them the expense of hiring an outside accountant."

"I never knew Dad was a CPA." Despite being furious with her missing father, she experiences a sense of longing for him. So many things she meant to ask him but never did. Will she ever get the chance to talk to him again?

"He was very good with numbers, which is why I let him handle our finances."

"This is a nightmare, Mom. Why would Dad do this to us?"

Birdie exits out of the internet browser and spins around in her chair. "According to you, he left because of me. At least that's what you said yesterday. What did you mean by that?"

Hannah toys with a strand of her long mahogany hair. "Whatever I said yesterday was wrong. He left because of another woman."

Birdie stands to face her. "But you didn't know about the other woman yesterday when you said it. Admit it. You blame me for his disappearance. You think I drove him into the arms of another woman."

"You're his wife. Kids aren't usually the ones who destroy their parents' marriages." Hannah turns her back on her mother. "I'm hungry. I'm going to fix breakfast."

Birdie watches her daughter leave the room. She already knows why Cary turned away from her. But she desperately needs validation—the words spoken aloud from her daughter's lips. She chokes back a sob as the enormity of her new circumstances overcomes her. Cary stole money from his firm, cleaned out their bank accounts, and ran off with another woman. Not to mention her unmarried daughter is having a baby and doesn't even know who the father is. Birdie might handle one of these problems, but the combination is too much to bear. She's furious. And heartbroken. And dejected. Tears flood her eyes and stream down her cheeks. She needs a drink, but she left the vodka in the kitchen.

She finds Hannah at the stove, forking bacon out of a frying pan onto a paper towel.

Glancing over her shoulder at Birdie, Hannah asks, "What do you want on your omelet?"

"I'm not really hungry. But thanks."

"Neither of us ate anything yesterday, Mom. You have to keep up your strength."

Keep up my strength for what? she thinks. *Life as I know it is over.* But admitting that will not get Hannah off her back. "You're right. I'll have some cheddar cheese, please."

While Hannah is busy at the stove, Birdie pours two fingers of vodka in a juice glass and fills it the rest of the way with orange juice.

"I saw that, Mom," Hannah says.

Birdie returns the juice to the refrigerator and slams the door. "And I thought parents were the only ones who have eyes in the backs of their heads. Oh, wait. I forgot. You're a parent-in-training."

Hannah slides an omelet out of the pan, adds two slices of bacon, and shoves the plate at Birdie. "Considering the circumstances, drinking before breakfast would be understandable. But this isn't new for you, is it? Do you drink *every* morning before breakfast?"

"No. I don't drink *every* morning. I drink *most* mornings."

Hannah turns her back on Birdie, pouring scrambled eggs into the pan for her omelet.

Birdie takes the plate to the table and waits for Hannah to join her before taking a bite. When the eggs hit her stomach like a wrecking ball, she throws up a little in her mouth and drowns the taste of bile with the rest of her screwdriver.

Hannah eyes her empty glass. "You do a good job of hiding it, but it's obvious you have a drinking problem. I learned about people like you in my freshman psychology class. You're a functioning alcoholic. I begged Dad to stage an intervention. But he either refused to accept or preferred to ignore your problem."

"Because it isn't serious. I can quit today." Birdie snaps her fingers for effect.

Hannah stuffs a forkful of eggs into her mouth. "Then why don't you?"

"Fine. I will." Birdie takes the bottle to the sink and pours the vodka down the drain.

"We'll see how long that lasts," Hannah says under her breath.

Birdie just opened the bottle, and a lot of precious liquid goes to waste. Fortunately, she has other bottles hidden in the cabinet in the laundry room and under the sink in the downstairs powder room. But from now on, thanks to Cary, she must be more frugal.

She returns to the table, but she doesn't touch her food. She watches her daughter gobble down every morsel of her breakfast, as though she's been deprived of food for a month. Pregnancy. The thought has no sooner entered Birdie's mind when Hannah leaps to her feet and makes a dash for the bathroom. When she emerges ten minutes later, the color has drained from her face and beads of sweat dot her forehead. What is wrong with Birdie that she feels no compassion for her daughter?

"I was sick every single day during my pregnancy with you. Even so, a baby is much easier to care for in the womb. You have other options besides abortion, adoption being one of them."

"I don't want to talk about this right now." Hannah walks her plate to the sink, rinses it, and stores it in the dishwasher.

"That's the thing, though. You don't take care of a child when it's convenient for you. Being a parent is a full-time job." The smell of bacon and eggs sends another wave of nausea crashing over Birdie, and she pushes the plate away. "Have you thought about how you're going to support yourself and a baby? You can't count on me to help, now that your father has run off with all of our money. I paid your tuition for the spring in full, but I'm not sure I can even afford the rent on your apartment."

"Don't sweat it. I can figure out a way to pay my rent." Hannah returns the eggs, milk, and cheese to the refrigerator and slams the door shut. "I'm twelve hours shy of earning a degree in cyber security. I'm not worried about finding a job after graduation."

Birdie takes her frustration and anger out on her paper

napkin, shredding it into pieces on the table. "Being a parent is hard enough when you have a spouse to support you. And you're so young. You've worked so hard in school. You need to enjoy young adulthood. You'll never get these years back."

Crossing the room, Hannah pauses in the doorway, but she doesn't look back at Birdie. "I don't want or need your advice, Mom. You and I have never been close. Dad has always been my go-to parent. You can't suddenly take his place now that he's gone."

Upstairs in her room, Hannah neatly folds her clothes into her suitcase. Thinking ahead, she includes the loose-fitting dresses and oversized tunics she bought after she gained ten pounds her freshman year from drinking beer and eating late-night pizza. As she places her new DSLR camera and telephoto lens, both Christmas gifts from her dad, into her camera bag, she can't help but wonder if he purchased the photography equipment with money stolen from his law firm. The camera is a source of income for her. She can't . . . she won't give it back now.

Gathering her toiletries from the hall bathroom, she tosses her cosmetic bag into her suitcase and zips it closed. Hannah's phone rings on the bed, and she glances down at the screen. She longs to talk to her best friend, to tell Liza about the baby and her dad. Liza is patient and understanding and nonjudgmental. But she's also perfect, beautiful and smart. Liza would never have forgotten to take her birth control pills. She would never be stupid enough to get pregnant. Liza has been calling and texting throughout the break, but Hannah's been blowing her off. And she lets the call go to voice mail now.

Hannah takes a last look around her childhood bedroom, at the Taylor Swift poster on the wall, the dollhouse under the window, the lacrosse stick and tennis racket in the corner. She no longer has use for any of these items. She was never an athlete, and the little girl who once played with dolls and idolized female pop singers is now on the verge of becoming an adult.

Slinging her backpack and camera bag over her shoulder, she wheels her suitcase out of the room and down the stairs where she finds her mother still sitting at the kitchen table.

Birdie's face melts when she sees her suitcase. "Where're you going?"

"Back to school."

Birdie rises from the table and walks toward her. "But classes don't start for another week."

"I'll use the time to get settled and ready for the semester. My roommates aren't back yet, and I really need to be alone right now."

Birdie grabs her arm. "Please, don't go," she says in a desperate tone. "I need you here with me. We can work through this together."

"There's nothing to work through, Mom. Dad is gone. Our home is broken."

When Hannah moves toward the front door, Birdie tightens her grip on her arm. "Will you at least seek counseling about the pregnancy?"

Hannah glares at her mother. "If you'll seek counseling for your drinking problem."

Birdie lets go of her arm.

"I thought so." Grabbing her suitcase handle, Hannah hurries out the front door, leaving it open behind her. Her chest feels heavy, and she finds it difficult to breathe. She wants her mother to follow her, to beg her to stay. She slows her pace and takes her time stowing her bags in the back of her red Jeep Wrangler, another gift from her dad. But Birdie remains in the house.

Hannah starts the engine and heads off down the driveway. With one last glance in the rearview mirror, she sees her mother standing in the doorway, waving goodbye. What will become of

Birdie? What will become of Hannah? If only they could travel back in time a week. What she would give to relive Christmas Day. Their family wasn't perfect. All families have their problems. But at least they were a family. Now they are three people going their separate ways.

THREE

Birdie waits in the doorway long after her daughter pulls out of the driveway and disappears down the road. Until freezing drizzle pings her face and drives her inside. She camps out at the kitchen table with her cell phone in front of her, willing it to ring or ping with a call or text from Cary. From this vantage point, she can see the front door, the door leading to the garage, and the dock. While common sense tells her he's not coming back, her heart holds out hope he'll walk through the door with a logical explanation about his whereabouts over the past two days. She might forgive him his affair with a mystery woman, but she would never get over him embezzling funds from his law office. What was it Jonathan said? *I've known Cary all my life, and one day, you'll understand how much better off you are without him.* Birdie's known Cary for thirty years. How could she have been that wrong about him? Is her ability to judge character that flawed? If she's better off without him, why does it hurt so much?

Throughout the afternoon and early evening, Birdie takes periodic shots of vodka, not to get drunk but to maintain the numbness that allows her to endure the ache in her chest. She's lost her husband. Her daughter can't stand the sight of her. And, unless the sprawling live oak in her front yard sprouts hundred-dollar bills come spring, she will soon lose her home. She longs to call Max, her lifelong best friend. But pride prevents her from clicking on the number. Max is so accomplished, so strong and capable. While Birdie is a complete and utter failure at life.

Year by year, decade by decade, Birdie relives her life. She was the quintessential stay-at-home mom when Hannah was young. She planned elaborate birthday parties and organized play dates. She went on school field trips and served as a room parent. All that changed when Hannah entered middle school and began cultivating her own social life. It was also around that time when she developed an interest in boating and kayaking and wildlife photography, outdoor activities that drew Hannah away from Birdie and closer to her father.

Birdie hadn't minded so much. Her heart had swelled with love at the sight of Hannah and her father paddling off together at daybreak with their cameras. During Hannah's high school years, Birdie, with few hobbies or interests to occupy her time, had grown lonely and bored. And she'd begun to eagerly antici-pate her afternoon cocktails.

Birdie counts seven hours off the clock—driving time to Richmond plus extra for traffic slow-downs and stops for food and gas. She sends Hannah a text. *Back safely?*

Hannah immediately responds with a curt *yes*.

Birdie takes to her bed for the next five days. Sleep doesn't come easily, but when it does, she has nightmares and night sweats. She wakes with clammy skin and excruciating headaches. She has no appetite and eats little, bits of leftovers from Christmas dinner that are long since past their prime—slices of honey-baked ham and a spoonful of sweet potato casserole.

Late morning on the sixth day, she wakes to find Max

standing over her. "How did you get in?" she asks, gripping the covers to her chest.

Max holds up a blue plastic key ring from which dangles a silver house key. "You gave me this ten years ago, when you asked me to feed your goldfish while the three of you were at Disney World over spring break." Max lowers herself to the edge of the bed. "I intentionally stayed away thinking you needed some time to yourself. I see that I was wrong. You look like hell, and you smell godawful. When's the last time you bathed?"

"I don't remember." Birdie squeezes her eyes tight against the bright sunshine streaming in through the window. "Close the blinds, already. My head hurts."

"Probably because you're hungry. When's the last time you ate anything?"

"I've eaten."

"But not a proper meal?" Max asks, and Birdie shakes her head.

Max strokes her arm. "Oh, honey. I'm so sorry. Is what they're saying about Cary true?"

Tears leak from the corners of Birdie's eyes and roll down the sides of her face. With quivering chin, she says, "He took all our money and ran off with another woman."

"And the part about him embezzling funds from the firm?"

How did that get out? Birdie wonders. Jonathan would never have betrayed her. "All true."

"Where's Hannah?" Max asks.

"She's gone back to school. She hates me, too." Birdie rolls over on her side away from Max. "Please, just go. I wanna be alone."

"No way I'm leaving you." Jumping to her feet, Max yanks back the covers. "Get up. After you shower and dress, we're going to have a nice long talk while we eat lunch. I brought over some homemade vegetable beef stew."

Birdie balls up into a fetal position. "Seriously, Max. Go away."

"Not a chance." Max is strong for such a tiny person. She grabs Birdie by the ankles and drags her legs over the side of the bed. When her feet hit the floor, she takes hold of her wrists and pulls her to a standing position.

Dizziness overcomes her, and Birdie stumbles backward. "Easy now." Hooking an arm around her waist, Max walks Birdie into the adjoining bathroom.

While Max adjusts the shower controls, Hannah, gripping the marble countertop, studies her reflection in the mirror above the sink. The haunted woman staring back at her makes her weak in the knees.

"There now. I think that's about right." Max turns away from the shower to face Birdie. "Do you want me to help you undress?"

When Max tugs at her nightgown, Birdie swats her hand away. "I can do it. I'm not an invalid," she says, despite feeling like one. She wants to shrivel up and die in her bed. Max is the only one who would miss her.

"Okay, then. I'll be in the kitchen heating up the soup. Call me if you need me." Max exits the bathroom, leaving the door open on her way out.

Birdie stands under the steaming shower until her fingers wrinkle, and the water runs cold. Feeling slightly revived, she slips on her terrycloth robe and goes to the kitchen. Max has set two places at the table, and seated across from each other, they eat in silence.

Birdie, despite the persistent nausea, devours the meal—flavorful beef and vegetable soup, sweet potato biscuits, and a salad of baby green lettuces, chunks of juicy pear, and blue cheese crumbles. Max is an excellent cook, her culinary skills honed from years of entertaining guests at the boutique hotel she owns and operates.

Max pops the last of a biscuit in her mouth and sits back in her chair. "Tell me about Hannah. When did she leave?"

"The day after Cary disappeared. You know what a daddy's girl she is. She wanted to lick her wounds in private."

Max studies Birdie more intently. "What are you not telling me? Did the two of you have a fight?"

"In a manner of speaking." Birdie balls up her napkin and throws it on the table. "She's pregnant, Max."

Max gasps. "Oh, God, no. Not Hannah."

"She's determined to keep the baby. I pointed out that she has options. But she didn't want to hear them. I can't support her in this decision. Not when she's throwing her life away. She'll only be twenty-two years old and raising a baby on her own. She doesn't even know who the father is."

Deep lines appear on Max's forehead. "I don't believe that. Hannah's not the type to . . ." Her voice trails off.

"To what? To sleep around? I didn't think so either, but she did."

Max rises from the table and begins gathering their dishes. "Poor Hannah. She must feel so alone. And to have her father abandon her when she needs him the most."

Birdie stands to face her. "I've got this, Max." She takes the dishes Max holds. "Thanks so much for coming over. I really needed a solid meal. But I'm feeling tired. I think I'll take a nap."

Max narrows her eyes, scrutinizing her, as though deciding whether Birdie is fit to be left alone. "Fine. But I'll be checking in on you every day. You need your friends right now. I'm here for you, Birdie. Let me help."

Birdie takes the dishes to the sink. "I will. When I'm ready. But I'm still numb. I'm struggling to wrap my mind around everything that's happened."

"You should get counseling. I can give you the name of my therapist. She really helped me after Daniel died."

"Maybe in a few weeks." The only counseling Birdie needs is 80 proof and a heck of a lot cheaper than a shrink.

"Look on the bright side. You have your pie business to keep you busy. And you've been talking about expanding your line of baked goods. Now might be the perfect time."

"Maybe."

Max puts on her coat, and they walk to the front door together. Birdie holds out her hand. "Can I have my key back? I don't want you sneaking into my house again while I'm sleeping."

"Sorry. I'm keeping the key for now." Max pats her handbag at her hip. "If you return my phone calls and answer the door when I knock, I won't have to use it."

Hannah relishes the time alone in the row house she rents with three other girls in Richmond's Fan District near the VCU campus. She feels safe, locked away in her third-floor bedroom. On her first night back, she cries herself to sleep, the sound of her sobs echoing throughout the empty house. But the next morning she wakes angry as hell. Hannah had nothing to do with her parents' marital problems. Why is *she* being punished? Why is her dad taking it out on her?

None of it makes any sense. Hannah and her dad are tight. Wouldn't she have known if he was unhappy? If he was having an affair? Then a thought occurs to her. What if her father didn't abandon her? What if he's waiting for the dust to settle before getting in touch with her?

This newfound hope gets Hannah through the days that follow. Her phone becomes a permanent extension of her hand as she goes about her business. She meets with her faculty adviser to discuss career options, puts in a request for extra hours at the Campus Coffee shop where she's worked part-time for the past two years, and posts notifications on various bulletin boards offering her services as tutor for a variety of subjects from Calculus 101 to writing computer code.

It snows four inches midweek, and early the following morning, Hannah goes out with her new camera to explore. But none of her pictures are worth saving. Her subjects are uninspiring, the winter landscape bleak despite the glorious morning sunlight. She wishes she could blame her new camera. True, she's not yet familiar with many of the different features. But her father's disappearance has thrown her perspective on the world off-kilter.

Hannah's roommates arrive late in the afternoon on Friday. Squeals of laughter and loud music drift up two flights of stairs to her bedroom. Kayla barges into her room around eight. "What up, girlfriend? Why are you hiding out up here all alone? Get dressed. We're going to Social 52."

Hannah glances up from her laptop. Kayla, the prettiest of the roommates with long blonde hair and sparkly blue eyes, is dressed for sex in a black, clingy, super-short dress and over-the-knee boots. "Ya'll go ahead without me. I'm not really in the mood to go out."

Kayla smacks her knee. "Since when, party girl? Ryan's going to be there."

Hannah groans. "Now I know I'm not going."

Kayla plops down on her bed at Hannah's feet. "Are you seriously still mad at him?"

Mad doesn't begin to describe how Hannah feels about her ex-boyfriend. "The anger has faded a little, but I'm still hurt and disappointed."

"Ryan texted me a lot over break. He feels awful about what happened, and he misses you like crazy." Kayla gives her leg a shove. "Forgive him already and get on with it. The two of you are meant to be together."

"If he cared about me, he wouldn't have cheated on me."

"Jeez, Hannah! Stop being such a drama queen. He only

kissed that girl. He didn't sleep with her or anything. He was drunk."

"That's no excuse." Hannah is surprised when her throat thickens, and tears threaten. She thought she was over the worst of her breakup with Ryan.

Rolling off the bed, she slips her computer in her backpack, puts on her down coat, and stuffs her feet in snow boots.

"Where are you going?" Kayla asks, watching her.

"I have to work," she says, and leaves the room without looking back.

Outside on the sidewalk, she takes deep icy breaths to steady her nerves. She walks aimlessly toward campus. She considers going to the library, but it's Friday night and classes haven't even started yet. When she finds herself in front of Campus Coffee, even though she's not on the schedule to work, she ducks inside.

She orders a decaf from a counter clerk she doesn't recognize and claims a table by the window. She tries to focus on updating her resume, but clusters of students laughing and cutting up as they pass by on the sidewalk distract her. Forcing her gaze away from the window, she studies the handful of students in the coffee shop. She spots Chris, a Chinese guy she knows from her computer science classes, at the counter. She locks eyes with him, and when he finishes paying for his drink, he comes over to her table and sits down opposite her without being invited.

"What're you doing here on a Friday night?" Chris asks.

"Working on my resume. What about you?"

"I'm doing some preliminary networking before starting the interview process." He blows on his coffee before taking a sip. "Why aren't you off partying somewhere with your friends?"

"I'm tired of college and over the party scene. Bring on the real world." Despite being pregnant and moping about her dad, she's genuinely ready to move on with her life.

"Aren't you a cyber security major?" When she nods, he asks, "What companies are you hoping to get interviews with?"

"I'm not sure yet. I'm still doing research. What about you?" She studies Chris as he talks about the firms he's interested in. He's kinda cute in his red plaid flannel shirt. Behind rectangular black eyeglass frames, his brown eyes are warm, and something about his smile sets her at ease.

"Where do you wanna live?" she asks.

"California. My girlfriend from back home goes to school out there."

"Back home, as in China?"

"Yes, China. My proper name is Wang Xiu Ying. Chris is the American name I adopted. My parents are poor farmers. I'm an only child. They spent their life savings sending me to college in the states. I haven't seen them or my girlfriend in almost four years, since I came here my freshman year."

Hannah experiences a pang of guilt for being so mean to her mom. "You must miss them a lot."

Sadness crosses his face. "Very much."

Hannah closes her laptop, suddenly more interested in his life than her resume. "What do you do over the holidays with no family around?"

Chris chuckles. "I work at the Apple Store. Come Christmas, I'm usually too exhausted to be lonely. What about you?" He tilts his head to the side as he studies her. "Let me guess. Wealthy family. Privileged background."

Wealthy? No. Comfortable? Once. "Everything about my life is average. Except that I'm from coastal South Carolina. Living on the water is the privilege."

Hannah had never realized until that moment how much the inlet means to her. She'll miss the wildlife when she takes a job in Atlanta or New York. Or maybe even California. Hannah wonders what it would be like to live on the West Coast where she knows no one. The idea intrigues her, and she adds California to her list to research for job opportunities.

They talk for another two hours. They share many of the

same interests—computers and photography and political views. Chris is unlike her girlfriends, who are only interested in boys, fashion, and partying. Besides, he has a girlfriend, which makes him a safe zone for Hannah. Romance is the last thing she needs right now. Not that anyone would be interested in a twenty-two-year-old unmarried pregnant girl.

FOUR

Hannah's friendship with Chris gets her through the desolate weeks of January. He's in three of her four classes, and whenever they're not working at their part-time jobs, they're studying together in the library. They attend resume writing and interview preparation seminars. During the second week of classes, they go to their first campus job fair. Hannah becomes increasingly more interested in moving to California, where the leading firms are located. Being so far from home appeals to Hannah. Away from her mother. Away from Ryan. Neither Hannah nor Chris is surprised when they find themselves attracted to the same firms. When they set up interviews with the company representatives, Chris, in a teasing tone, says, "Let the best man win."

"Or woman," she adds, sending an elbow to his ribs.

Hannah has never been close friends with a guy before. He's upfront about most things, and she always knows where she stands with him. He's a good listener, and she tells him about Ryan and her father's mysterious disappearance. But she doesn't feel comfortable telling him about the baby.

On weekends, Hannah and Chris go on early morning photo

shoots, and he shows her how to use the features on her new camera. The quality of her photographs improves, and she makes some of her best shots available for purchase on stock image websites. The earnings are meager, but combined with tutoring and her income from the coffee shop, she's able to support herself without having to ask her mother for money.

Hannah hears nothing from her dad, and when she places the obligatory Sunday evening calls to her mom, Birdie's speech is slurred and her thoughts confused. The conversation ends the same way every time. When her mother harasses Hannah about having an abortion, Hannah hangs up on her.

Hannah asks herself repeatedly if she's doing the right thing by seeing the pregnancy through. Every time her answer is an unequivocal yes. She believes every woman has the right to make decisions regarding her own body. But abortion isn't right for her. She loved Ryan, but she's not having his baby to hold on to him. The baby she carries is filling an emptiness that has been a part of her for as long as she can remember. At the end of January, when the deadline for her to have a safe abortion passes, she's relieved to give up that inner struggle.

Her roommates become increasingly bitchier toward Hannah when she rejects their many invitations to hang out and go to parties. On a Thursday night in mid-February, she arrives home from her shift at Campus Coffee to find her three roommates lined up on the sofa, wine glasses in hand, waiting for her.

"We need to talk." Kayla motions Hannah to the club chair with the red wine stain. Hannah can't remember who the chair belongs to, either Emma or Courtney, but she's certain Kayla is responsible for the stain.

Seated across from them, she feels as though she's the child and they are her parents, punishing her for sneaking out of the house. "What's up?"

"We're concerned about you, honey," Kayla says, and Emma and Courtney nod in unison. "And, quite frankly, our feelings are hurt. You never go out with us anymore. You spend all your time with that Chinese guy. Are you sleeping with him? Because, if you are, you'll never get Ryan back."

Hannah glares at Kayla. "I already told you, I don't want Ryan back. And I'm not sleeping with Chris. He has a longtime girlfriend. We're just friends."

Courtney falls back against the sofa cushion, the wine sloshing in her glass. "That's a relief. I thought maybe you'd gone off the deep end."

Kayla shoots Courtney a warning look. "That doesn't explain why you've been hanging out with him and not us."

Hannah has known this moment was coming. She has a choice. She can either tell them about the baby or her father. But she can't afford to have Ryan find out she's pregnant. She exhales loudly. "I haven't been myself lately. Something happened over Christmas, and I'm having a hard time dealing with it."

"What happened?" Emma says, leaning in closer, eager for details.

"My father left my mother," Hannah says, leaving out the part about him embezzling funds from his law firm and vanishing into the night with a mystery woman. "It's been hard. My mom's pretty broken up about it."

"Oh, sweetie, I'm so sorry." Emma's tone is genuine as is Courtney's when she adds, "Why didn't you tell us? You shouldn't have to suffer alone."

Kayla eyes Hannah suspiciously. "Does Chris know about this?"

Hannah lies, "I don't talk to Chris about personal stuff. We have the same major. He's in most of my classes. And he enjoys photography like me." This seems to satisfy them, and Hannah thinks she's off the hook, until Kayla goes into the kitchen and returns with a glass of red wine.

"Here." She slides the glass across the coffee table. "You need this."

"Thanks, but I have an early class in the morning." Hannah gathers her things and heads for the stairs.

Kayla calls after her, "You might wanna watch the carbs, Han. I know it's tempting to comfort eat during stressful times, but you're looking a little thick around the middle."

Their laughter follows her as she hurries up to the safety of her third-floor bedroom. Locking the door behind her, she flops down on the bed and sobs into her pillow. She must be extra careful to avoid her roommates for the rest of the semester. Classes end in early May. As a senior, she'll be exempt from exams, and she has no intention of staying for graduation. But she'll be twenty-six or twenty-seven weeks pregnant by then. She'll wear bulky sweaters, even on warm days. Under no circumstances can she let them find out about the baby.

———

Birdie has the same recurring nightmare every night. She's sinking in the murky water to the muddy bottom of the creek in front of her house. She tries to fight her way to the surface, but an invisible force keeps pulling her downward. She never drowns or swims to the surface. The struggle goes on and on until she awakens covered in sweat.

She understands what the dream means. She's drowning her sorrows in alcohol. But she's powerless to stop, no matter how much booze she pours down the drain or how many times she vows to quit drinking. She can go only a few hours before temptation strikes and she's on her way to the liquor store.

The weeks pass in a blur. Max is the only person Birdie sees. And she keeps her at bay as best she can. She responds to Max's texts and speaks to her through cracked doors when Max drops off food several times a week.

Birdie scours Cary's devices, searching for any electronic communications that might offer insight into his whereabouts.

But she comes up empty. She hasn't a clue what she'll do if she finds him. Have him arrested? Shoot him dead with his own shotgun?

She combs through his clothes. In his pockets, she finds a tube of lipstick, not Birdie's shade, and a black lace thong, which is not hers either. Perhaps that was part of their problems. Maybe she should've been wearing black thongs and sexy lingerie to spice up their love life. But Cary never showed he was bored with sex. Okay, that's not entirely true. In recent years he has become less interested in her body. But doesn't that happen to all middle-aged couples? Is that any reason for him to run off with another woman?

Late in the day on a Saturday afternoon toward the end of January, she lights a fire in an old oil drum on the brick patio and burns all of Cary's clothes, including his shoes, underwear, and socks.

Around the beginning of February, Birdie finally gives up hope of ever hearing from Cary again. He's probably in Tahiti, or some equally exotic foreign place, living the dream with his mystery woman. She barely misses him, anyway. Her depression, her need to drink, is brought on by the feeling of worthlessness that consumes her night and day.

Birdie's job as a parent is over. Her daughter, a grown young woman, has made it clear she's capable of making her own decisions by having a baby out of wedlock at twenty-two years of age. Hannah's pregnancy eats at Birdie. Not only is she frustrated with Hannah for throwing away her life, she's concerned about Hannah's health and the logistics of giving birth to the baby.

The bills pile up until Birdie fears the electrical company will turn off her power. Seated at her desk, she goes through them one by one, writing checks and submitting online payments. The American Express bill includes all their charges from Christmas. Her eyes pop when she sees how much Cary paid for Hannah's camera and telephoto lens. He then ran off with all their money, leaving Birdie to figure out how to pay for his extravagant gift to their daughter. In all their twenty-five years of marriage, she never realized he was such a jerk.

Birdie has twelve hundred dollars left after she pays the bills. With more bills arriving every day and no money coming in, she has no choice but to sell the house. The notion of losing her home sends her over the edge, and she drinks more that night than ever before. In a fit of rage, she ravages her family room with one of Cary's golf clubs. She breaks lamps and beats feathers out of throw pillows. She scars antique wooden furniture and breaks the glass in picture frames bearing their family photos.

She wakes the following morning to the sound of Max gasping. "What on earth? Who ransacked your house? Did someone break in last night?" Another gasp. "Birdie, what happened to your feet? There's blood everywhere."

Bleeding? That explains the pain. But what happened to them? She opens her eyes. The room spins, and she closes them again.

"Good lord," Max says, and Birdie hears a thunk, the sound of an object being placed on the coffee table near her head. "Did you drink this entire bottle of vodka? I'm calling an ambulance."

Without opening her eyes, Birdie's left hand shoots out and grabs the leg of Max's jeans. "Please, don't," she mumbles through parched lips.

"You need medical attention, if not for alcohol poisoning, then for your feet. They're cut to shreds."

"I'm fine. I just need a minute." Careful not to disturb her feet, Birdie props herself on one elbow. Blood from deep gashes in her feet soak the cushions at the other end of the sofa. She surveys the destruction in the room—broken lamps, overturned furniture, pages of books ripped to shreds, shards of glass from broken picture frames embedded in the carpet—the source of the cuts on her feet.

Max lowers herself to the edge of the coffee table. "How long has the drinking been a problem?"

Birdie rakes her fingers through her matted hair. This is bad. Really bad. This is rock bottom, the turning point. She either gets herself together now or . . . or what? She can't bring herself to think about the *or what.* "Years."

"In my limited experience with such things, it's pointless to force help on an alcoholic. They have to be willing to accept it. Are you willing?"

She nods, a tear trickling down her cheek. "I don't want to live like this."

Max pulls out her phone and thumbs the screen. "Then we need to get you into a good rehab program. There's—"

"No! Not rehab. I'll do better. I promise." She squeezes her eyes tight, but the tears keep coming. "I'm broke, Max. I have to sell the house. I'm scared, and I'm angry as hell at Cary. But I'm angry at myself, too, for letting this happen. I've lost everything. My family and now my home. I have nothing left to live for."

Max sets her phone down on the table beside her. "You've always talked about going back into nursing. Maybe now is the right time to do that."

Birdie shakes her head. "I let my license lapse. I would have to complete a reentry program. It's not worth it. I never loved nursing. The work is rewarding, but I no longer have the energy for the long shifts in the ER."

"What about your bakery business? People love your pies and you have plenty of opportunity to expand."

"Right. They love them so much, not a single person has requested a pie since New Year's."

"Because they understand you're having a family crisis, but several of your biggest fans have asked me when you're going to start baking again."

Birdie feels a flutter in her belly. Is that hope? It's been so long, she doesn't recognize it. "Really?"

"Yes, really." Max grabs her hand. "I'll make a deal with you. I'll move in here with you for a few days, but if you can't stay sober, you'll go to rehab."

Birdie rolls her head to the side to look at her friend. "But what about the hotel?"

"I closed for January and February to make some repairs. I can take a break from painting and tile work."

"If you help me get back on my feet, I'll help you finish your repairs."

"That's a deal I won't turn down," Max says with a smile. "You're a beautiful woman, Birdie. But you're even more beautiful when your inner light shines through. I haven't seen that light shine in a very long time, but I'm going to help you find it again."

FIVE

Max remains at Birdie's bedside through the worst of her alcohol withdrawal. She places cool washcloths on her forehead and changes the bandages on her wounded feet. When she feels like eating, Max brings her healthy meals on trays and counsels her through her many mood swings. Five days later, on a Friday afternoon, Birdie finally turns the corner and leaves her bedroom to find order restored to her family room.

"You're too good to me, Max." She roams the room, surveying the permanent damage. How could she not remember wreaking such havoc?

Max smiles. "You once did the same for me."

This is true. Birdie nurtured Max through the dark months following her husband's sudden death from a heart attack three years ago. Just as Max had been a strong shoulder for Birdie to cry on when both her parents were killed in a car accident fifteen years ago. "We've always been here for each other."

"And we always will." Max takes Birdie's hand. "Let's get some fresh air." She leads Birdie through the kitchen and out the back door.

The day is warm with bright blue skies, and Birdie feels like a bear emerging from its cave after a long winter. "What's the date, Max?"

"February twenty-fourth."

Birdie cocks an eyebrow. "Seriously? My life is passing me by in a blur."

Max nods. "I know what you mean. Our time on earth is precious. We shouldn't waste a single day. And I'm here to make sure you don't waste any more of yours."

Still holding hands, they mosey down to the water and out to the end of the dock. Breathing in deeply, Birdie says, "How will I give all this up?"

"You'll find something new. Your next stage of life is waiting for you out there"—she spreads her arms wide at the inlet—"in this great, big, beautiful world."

Birdie places her hand over her racing heart. "You and Daniel were married for twenty years. You know how terrifying it is to move into the next stage of life without the man you thought you'd grow old with."

Max turns toward the house. "I never said it'd be easy. Think of it as an adventure. Your home is lovely, and waterfront properties are a hot commodity. You'll have no trouble selling it. With no mortgage to pay off, you can put the money in the bank. Your only child is grown, and with no husband or house tying you down, you can do whatever you want."

Birdie remains facing the water. What she wants is her old life back. She's poured her heart and soul into taking care of this house. "But my only child grew up here. How will I let those memories go?"

"Those memories don't live in this house. They live in your heart. They will be with you always, wherever you go." Taking her hand, Max drops to the edge of the dock and pulls Birdie down beside her. "Think of your future as a clean slate from which to start over. Consider it a gift. You can travel. Move to a new town. Go back to school and learn a new trade."

"I love Palmetto Island. I'm a South Carolinian, born and raised. Where else would I go?"

"Wherever Hannah lands. Wouldn't you like to be near her, to help take care of the baby?"

Birdie experiences a pang of guilt. While she fully expects Hannah to move to another city after graduation, she never once considered leaving Palmetto Island to be near her. As for the baby, she doesn't think of it as her grandchild. It's an obstacle that will prevent Hannah from having a normal life. "You didn't follow Kyle when he moved to New York," she argues.

"Me?" She thumbs her chest. "In New York City? I love my son, but no thank you. I'll never leave the Lowcountry."

"Hannah doesn't want me around. She wants her daddy back."

"I'm sure she does, but it doesn't look like he's coming back. Now's your chance to grow closer to Hannah. Every woman needs her mother when she's having her first baby."

Birdie rests her head against the dock piling. "I wish I knew how to get through to her. How did you manage to have such a healthy relationship with Kyle?"

Max stares up at the cloudless sky as she considers her answer. "Being a parent of a young adult isn't easy. They're making decisions that will impact the rest of their lives, yet you can't offer advice unless they ask for it. You let them chart their own course, even if they're headed for disaster. When they fall, and they will fall, you be there to pick them up."

Birdie has a lot to learn about parenting. As for her daughter keeping this baby, she's not sure she can hold her tongue.

A comfortable silence settles over them as they watch pelicans dive for fish nearby. "Do you think my bakery business has a chance?" Birdie asks.

"Absolutely. Not only are you an excellent cook, you're great at marketing. Those adorable emails you send out are impossible to ignore." Max tucks her right foot beneath her left leg as she angles her body toward Birdie. "Although, playing devil's advocate here, we already have one bakery. I'm not sure our town is big enough for two. Then again, Amber's pies aren't nearly as good as yours."

"I wasn't thinking of opening a bakery, Max. I would continue cooking pies out of my home." The inescapable feeling of doom comes crashing back. "Soon, I won't have a home with a kitchen to cook in."

When Birdie gets up slowly and walks gingerly on sore feet toward the house, Max calls after her, "Where're you going?"

Birdie yells over her shoulder, "Up to the house. I need to check on something."

In the office, she opens the bottom, right-hand drawer where they store their important documents in hanging files. She removes the one pertaining to their mortgage and opens it on the desk. Her eyes grow wide as she thumbs through the pages. Cary made their last mortgage payment in October. Birdie already knew this. They celebrated with a dinner out and too much wine for Birdie. According to the paperwork, when the bank transferred the deed back to them, he made certain hers was the only name listed on the document. This makes her feel better, at the same time so much worse. While he'd depleted their savings and brokerage accounts, he provided for her in another way, to the tune of a half-million dollars at today's market value. But this also means that since October—and who knows how long before that—while Birdie had been doing his laundry and cooking his meals and kissing him goodnight, he'd been planning to escape town with another woman.

Late in the afternoon on a Thursday during the first week of March, Hannah exits the coffee shop to find Ryan waiting for her on the sidewalk out front. Her first thought is one of relief that she's wearing a down vest to hide her expanding midsection.

"We need to talk." He takes her arm and pulls her out of the way of a cluster of students hurrying past.

Hannah jerks her arm away. "There's nothing to talk about."

"I miss you. Will you consider giving me another chance? Please."

She can't bring herself to look at his adorable face, his white-blond hair, clear blue eyes, and irresistible dimples. Will their baby be fair like him or have brown hair and green eyes like her? "What's the point, Ryan? We're both graduating. We'll probably never see each other again."

He moves in close enough to smell his old spice body wash. "I thought we had something special."

Hannah snorts. "I thought so, too, until you cheated on me."

"I kissed her one time, Hannah. And she came on to me."

"I saw you with her, Ryan. That was more than one kiss. The two of you were practically having sex on the dance floor."

"We were drunk. I don't even know that girl's name."

"Ha. Like that's supposed to make me feel better. I've gotta go. I'm meeting someone at the library." She starts off down the sidewalk.

He steps in line beside her. "Who're you meeting? Your Chinaman?"

She glares at him out of the corner of her eye. "I find that offensive, Ryan. Not that it's any of your business, but Chris is my friend. He's helped me through a hard time."

"I heard about your father. I'm sorry. Divorce sucks."

Divorce she can handle. Abandonment is another matter entirely. "Who told you? Kayla?"

He hangs his head. "Yeah. She told me a few weeks ago."

She stops at an intersection, waiting for the crossing light to change. "A few weeks ago, and it's taken you this long to say anything to me? Oh wait. I forgot. You've been busy hooking up with Becky Sandler. Are you cheating on *her* now by trying to get back with me?"

The light changes, and Hannah takes off across the intersection before he can answer.

He catches up with her. "Becky and I aren't together. You're the one I care about, Hannah."

"You have a funny way of showing it." As they approach the library, Hannah slows her pace. She wants to prolong their time together, to give him every opportunity to say the magic words. The three words she needs to hear in order to give him another chance.

Instead of telling her he loves her, he asks, "What are your plans for after graduation?"

"I'm applying for a bunch of different jobs. I haven't settled on anything specific yet. What about you?" She's not interested in his future. She wants to know where he'll be so she can keep her baby as far away from him as possible.

"I'm studying to take the LSAT. I'll work for my father until I go to law school next year."

Their fathers are both attorneys, only her father is an ambulance chaser and his is the attorney general of South Carolina. "Good for you. Have a nice life, Ryan."

She feels his gaze on her back as she enters the library. She wills herself not to cry as she makes her way to the study area. Chris can tell right away that something is wrong. "Did you have another fight with your mom?"

Sniffling, she shakes her head. "I saw Ryan just now. He begged me to give him another chance."

Chris furrows his brow behind rectangular glasses. "Did you?"

"No way." She digs through her backpack for a travel pack of tissues. "But I'm glad I ran into him. Now I know for certain that whatever we had is over."

"Closure is a good thing, especially when you're looking for jobs in multiple cities."

"Speaking of jobs. I've been waiting to hear from Sandman Cyber Security." She opens her laptop on the desk, scrolls through her email, and lets out a squeal. "I got a final interview with them for next week."

"So did I," he says with a smirk on his lips.

She play-punches his arm. "Of course, you did."

"May the best man—"

She throws her pen at him. "Dude, the best woman's gonna win this time."

Even though Chris is an all-around better candidate for the job, she's determined to give this interview everything she's got. The signing bonus and large starting salary will enable her to provide a comfortable lifestyle for her baby despite California's high cost of living. And she'll be so far away Ryan will never find her.

SIX

Hannah's job interview with Sandman goes better than expected. She hits it off with Jeff Brandon, the senior executive in charge of interviewing potential candidates. She's confident in answering his many questions, and when they discuss potential start dates, she suggests September because of a previously planned trip to Europe with her family. She feels guilty for lying, but she doesn't worry about giving Chris the advantage over her. He, too, will travel over the summer to visit his parents in China.

Hannah interviews with a half dozen other firms, all of which have their headquarters in California. While Sandman remains at the top of her list, three others are definitely in the running.

The last weeks of Hannah's spring semester pass quickly. When she's not prepping for interviews or presenting projects, she's tutoring and working overtime at the coffee shop. She stays busy so as not to dwell on the changes taking place around her. Spring fever has struck the other students. They skip classes and rock the campus well into the night. The senior class appears equally divided between those frantically searching for jobs and those who seem unconcerned about what comes next for them. Her roommates fall in the latter category.

Hannah has become a persona non grata within her friend group. Behind her back but loud enough for Hannah to hear, her roommates make fun of her weight gain and say derogatory things about Chris. Hannah tells herself their opinion doesn't matter, but their comments cut deep nonetheless.

Hannah is careful to hide her baby bump, and to the unsuspecting eye, she's merely put on a few extra pounds. Despite the time they spend together, Chris doesn't notice her bump until a Friday afternoon in mid-April. They are down by the James River on Belle Isle experimenting with photographing water movement. They've mounted their cameras on tripods, and she's bent over hers, making adjustments in pursuit of the perfect shot. The April sun, warm on her back, causes sweat to dampen her armpits, and she strips off her down vest and tosses it on the ground without thinking.

"Whoa!" Chris says. "Hannah, are you pregnant?"

She looks up from her camera. His eyes are on her belly, her T-shirt stretched tight across her bump. She straightens, her hands dropping from the camera to her sides. "Please don't tell anyone."

"Is it Ryan's baby?"

"Yes," she says, her words barely audible over the sound of water rushing over rocks.

A concerned expression falls over his face. "Does he know?"

She shakes her head. "And I'm not telling him."

Their cameras forgotten, they move to the shade of a tree and sit down side-by-side on the ground.

"Ryan is your baby's father, Hannah. You have an obligation to tell him about his child."

Hannah hugs her knees to her chest. "Ryan doesn't care about me. And he won't care about our baby. Besides, he's going to law school, and I don't want to wreck his life. I decided to have this baby for me, not for him."

"What about when your baby gets old enough to question who its father is?"

She rests her chin on her knees. "I'll make up something. I'm not worried about that now."

"Is this why you can't start work until September?" When she doesn't answer, he adds, "You're not going to Europe this summer, are you?"

She shakes her head. "The baby is due in early August."

"Surely you're not planning to stay in Richmond. You can't have a baby alone."

"I'm waiting to find out about jobs. I may head out to California early. I've always wanted to drive across country. Now may be my only chance."

Chris shakes his head, as though he misheard her. "You can't drive across country alone."

"Sure, I can," she says with more conviction than she feels. "But I'll probably just go home to South Carolina for the summer. *If* my mom will let me. She's not thrilled about the baby."

"I'm sure." Chris pulls his phone out of his pocket and accesses Ryan's VCU profile. "Wait. Ryan's middle name is Augustus? Who would do that to their child?"

Hannah shrugs. "I kinda like it."

Chris thumbs his phone screen. "And he's from South Carolina. How's that gonna work? Your mom lives in a vacation hotspot. Before long, you won't be able to hide your pregnancy."

Hannah has spent sleepless nights worrying about this logistical detail. "I never met any of Ryan's friends from Columbia. And his family goes to Pawley's Island every summer, which is hours away from Palmetto Island. I'll hide out in my house if I have to. I realize it's a risk, and I don't have all the answers. I'm taking it one day at a time." She rubs her baby mound. "All I know for sure is that I love this baby, and I'm not giving him or her up."

Chris's phone rings, and he glances down at his screen. "It's a California number."

She shoulder-bumps him. "Answer it."

Scrambling to his feet, he steps away from her to accept the call.

She shifts on her bottom to see him, feeling a stab of envy when his face lights up. He got the Sandman job, and she's genuinely happy for him. Chris is a good guy, and he's worked hard. But she's disappointed. She'd viewed Sandman as her best chance. What if she doesn't get any offers? She'll be forced to look at firms in other cities. Places closer to Ryan.

When Chris rejoins her, his smile is broad. "Sandman offered me the job. I'm sorry, Hannah. I know how much you wanted it."

She flashes him a smile. "The best *man* won. Congratulations. I'm happy for you, Chris. You earned it."

When Hannah hears her cell phone ringing, she crawls across the ground to where she dropped her vest. Removing her phone from the pocket, she sees the call is also from a California number. When she answers, a familiar voice greets her. "Hannah, Jeff Brandon here. I'd like to offer you a job at Sandman."

"But . . . I'm here with Chris Ying and . . ."

Jeff chuckles. "You both made outstanding impressions on us. Since we're in expansion mode, we decided to offer jobs to both of you."

"That's incredible. I'm thrilled, Jeff. I accept." She punches the air, and Chris stands to face her, his expression eager.

"I'm thrilled to hear it. I'll email you the formal offer by the end of the day. Congratulations and welcome to the team."

Ending the call, she stares over at Chris. Her breath is shallow, her heart racing. "I can't believe it. The best *man* and *woman* won."

"Yay us!" Wrapping his arms around her, he lifts her slightly off the ground. He sets her down gently and drops his arms from around her waist. "I'm sorry, Hannah. I got carried away. I didn't hurt the baby, did I?"

Hannah laughs. "You didn't hurt the baby. I can't believe we're going to be working at the same firm."

"We should think about getting an apartment together. I can help out with the baby."

She imagines Chris trying to sleep after a long day at work and her colicky baby keeping him awake. "I appreciate the offer, but I'm not sure your girlfriend would approve."

Chris's face reddens. "You're probably right. But you won't be alone. I'll be there for you."

Hannah gasps when she feels a flutter in her belly. "I just felt the baby move for the first time." The pregnancy suddenly becomes real. Her baby is growing inside of her. She will never be alone again.

Moving into the spare bedroom in Max's top-floor apartment at the Palmetto Hotel provides Birdie the change of scenery she desperately needs. The fifty-room boutique hotel has been in Max's husband's family for generations. Max complains about her obligation to maintain the hotel, but Birdie knows she loves every minute. The customers who return year after year are testament to what a gracious host she is. The location is ideal—on the waterfront in the center of town, overlooking the marina and surrounded by seafood restaurants and charming boutiques. The view of the marsh from her bedroom window provides Birdie a calming reassurance that life as she's always known it isn't over.

Max puts Birdie in charge of painting the lobby. The physical exertion takes her mind off her problems and enables her to sleep at night. She loves the paint color Max has chosen—a lavender gray that reminds Birdie of a foggy morning on the inlet. While she works, she monitors through the plate-glass windows the constant stream of customers coming and going from the bakery on the other side of the small park that separates them. Maybe there is a future for her in baked goods after all.

A week passes, and then another and another. Birdie's feet heal and the craving to drink lessens. Together, Max and Birdie complete the minor renovations, but Birdie can't bring herself to return home, and Max offers for her to stay as long as she'd like. Birdie comes to realize her house is part of the problem. Max was right. The good memories are alive in her heart. But she sees the bad memories in the bed she once shared with her husband. In his hunting gear in the garage and his kayak on the rack down by the dock. In the bare spot on the wall in the family room where the photograph of Cary and Hannah hung before Birdie smashed the frame's glass with a golf club.

Birdie meets with the realtor and puts the house on the market. She has no remorse when she sees the For Sale sign in the front yard.

Birdie makes a shopping trip to the local Harris Teeter for a long list of ingredients and settles into the hotel's commercial kitchen for a bake-a-thon. She creates an assortment of tarts and pastries and scones, but she discovers she has a special knack for baking breads. She keeps detailed records of her recipes, tweaking the ingredients with each new batch.

As the days grow warmer, guests flock to the Palmetto Hotel on the weekends. In absence of a restaurant, a small lounge next to the lobby offers ample seating. Max readily turns over the responsibility of preparing the continental breakfast to Birdie.

On a Wednesday morning in mid-April, Birdie is covering the front desk for Max, when Amber from the bakery across the park enters the hotel.

"Where's Max?" Amber asks, her eyes darting around the lobby.

"At the dentist. Is there something I can help you with?"

Amber lets out a huff, as though Birdie will have to do in Max's absence. "I'm selling the bakery. My mother was diagnosed with pancreatic cancer, and I'm moving back home to take care of her."

What little Birdie knows about pancreatic cancer doesn't bode well for Amber's mother. "I'm sorry to hear that. But why sell? Can you get someone to run the bakery in your absence?" Birdie asks, her eyes twinkling.

Amber shakes her head. "I moved here ten years ago after my fiancé dumped me at the altar. I never planned to stay for so long. It's time for me to go home to Connecticut. I miss my family. Do you know anyone who might be interested in buying my business? I'll give them a fire-sale price. I need to get out in a hurry. Mom doesn't have much time."

Birdie comes around from behind the desk. "I may know just the person."

"The situation is ideal," Birdie says to Max later in the day when they are strolling along the boardwalk. "The upstairs apartment is small but charming. The commercial kitchen is state-of-the-art, and the price includes all the equipment and fixtures, which is too good to be real. The whole thing is too good to be real, now that I think about it. There must be a catch."

Max laughs. "There's no catch. Amber doesn't need money. Her family has plenty. She's desperate to get home to her mama."

Birdie presses her lips thin. "I see. That explains a lot."

"So, what's holding you back?"

Birdie shrugs. "I'd feel better if someone made an offer on my house."

They stop walking, and Max turns to Birdie. "Why don't you

ask Amber if you can manage the bakery until you sell your house?"

"That's actually a great idea. Do you think she'd go for it?"

"You never know until you ask. Go on. Call her."

Birdie narrows her blue eyes. "You mean now?"

"Yes! Amber is waiting to hear from you. If you're interested, you need to jump on this opportunity. The building, alone, is worth more than she's asking. Someone will gobble it up."

Birdie leans against the wooden railing with her back to the inlet. "I'm not sure I'm ready for such a big step."

"You're ready. Whether or not you know it. You've changed since you came to live with me. You're no longer a broken woman." Max's fingers graze Birdie's cheek. "The puffiness is gone from your face, and your skin has a healthy glow. But more than that, your inner light is once again shining through."

"Because I feel hopeful about my future for the first time in years."

As Birdie is staring at the phone in her hand, contemplating her conversation with Amber, her realtor's number flashes across the screen. When she answers, Shannon blurts, "We have a full price offer on the house, with no contingencies. Can you be out by mid-May?"

Birdie's hand shakes. So much has happened today. She could use a drink. The temptation creeps in at the most unexpected and inconvenient times. Will it ever go away completely?

"That's less than a month away," Birdie says. What will she do with all her furniture? Only a fraction of it will fit in the bakery apartment.

"That's not the right answer, Birdie," Shannon says in an irritated tone.

Birdie palms her forehead. "You're right. What am I thinking? I'll be out whenever you say. This is so exciting, Shannon. Thank you."

Shannon lets out a little laugh. "That's more like it." They talk for a minute about logistics before ending the call.

"Well?" Max asks, her blue eyes wide with curiosity.

"Full price. No contingencies. We close mid-May." Birdie inhales an unsteady breath. "I guess I'm buying a bakery."

Her phone rings again. "This is Hannah," Birdie says.

"Answer it. I need to get back to the hotel, anyway."

Waving goodbye to Max, Birdie accepts the call. "Hi, sweetheart. How are you?"

"Great! I got a job offer from my top choice."

"That's excellent news. Congratulations. When do you start?" She wants to ask how Hannah plans to launch her career with a newborn, but she holds her tongue.

"Not until September. The baby is due in early August."

Silence fills the line. Birdie can't think of anything to say that won't start a fight.

"So, Mom, the job's in San Diego."

"California?"

"Yes. California."

"But that's so far away," Birdie says as tears prick her eyelids. Her daughter's moving to California, all the way across the country.

"I was wondering . . . do you think I can come home for the summer? I'll get a job and pay rent."

Summer? Birdie thinks. *As in, she'll have the baby here in August.* If she says no, she may never see her daughter again. If she says yes . . . well, that could get complicated.

When Birdie doesn't respond, Hannah says, "I understand if you don't want me there. We didn't part on the best of terms."

"You can always come home, Hannah." Although her daughter won't be coming home to their house on the creek where Hannah grew up. She'll be returning to a two-bedroom apartment above a waterfront building. Birdie's mind races. She should tell Hannah about selling the house and buying the bakery. But that might scare her away. "Do you want me to come up for graduation? I could get Max to drive up with me." What is Birdie thinking? She hasn't been back to Richmond since drop-off day Hannah's freshman year. Why go now?

"I'm not walking at graduation. I'm exempt from exams. I'll be home as soon as my last class is over. Which will be sometime in early May. I'll text you when I find out the exact date."

"All right, then. I'll look forward to seeing you in May." Ending the call, Birdie moves to a nearby park bench and stares out at the boats in the marina. She has mixed emotions about her daughter coming home for the summer. Birdie has three months to make things right with her daughter. Closing her eyes, she prays to God she doesn't screw it up.

SEVEN

Hannah nearly drives her car up a tree when she sees the sign at the end of their driveway. How could her mother sell their home without telling her? She peels out in a fishtail of gravel as she speeds toward the house. She's relieved when her key still fits the front doorknob. She stomps down the hall to the family room, which is cluttered with stacks of books and china and miscellaneous odds and ends of furniture.

"What the heck, Mom?" she says to Birdie, who is placing price stickers on a set of *Encyclopedia Britannica.*

"Hannah!" Birdie gives her a stiff hug. "Welcome home."

"Clearly, it's no longer my home. I can't believe you sold our house."

"Your father left me no choice," Birdie says, returning to her task.

"If you're planning a yard sale, no one's going to buy those." She gestures at the encyclopedia collection.

Birdie lifts a shoulder in an unconcerned shrug. "You never know what people might buy at a yard sale."

"Where are we supposed to live?"

"In an apartment above the Island Bakery. I bought the entire building, business and all."

Hannah's eyebrows shoot up to her hairline. "You bought a bakery?" Her mother has gone off the deep end. The alcohol has pickled her brain. Although . . . on closer examination, Birdie doesn't appear drunk. Is she wearing makeup? And what's with the overalls? She looks younger. And happy.

"Amber, the woman who owned the bakery, had a family emergency and had to leave town suddenly. The deal was too good to pass up."

"Hey!" Hannah snatches up a small painting of an egret. "You can't sell this. I painted it in high school."

Birdie looks up from her sheet of stickers. "It's not for sale." She gestures at the assortment of kitchenware, furniture, and decorative items in the corner. "Those are all things I thought you might like to take with you to California. There's also a box of my old maternity clothes. I have no idea what's in there, but it might be worth a peek."

"No thanks on the maternity clothes. I'm managing fine with my yoga pants."

"You still have months to go. We'll take the box to the apartment, just in case."

Hannah rummages through the items. "I'd love to have some of this stuff for my apartment, but how will I get it to California?" Hannah realizes her mistake too late. She has graduated from college, and she's having a baby. She's supposed to be self-sufficient. Yet she hasn't given the first thought to the logistics of moving across country with a newborn.

"Maybe you should've thought of that before you accepted a job in California."

"Well, I didn't. Okay? If Dad were here, he'd rent a U-Haul and drive out with me."

"Since he's not here, we'll come up with another plan." Birdie folds her arms over her chest, the sheet of stickers dangling from her fingertips. "You could look into shipping them, although that's likely to be expensive. I've rented a miniwarehouse. The apartment is too small for all of our furniture. We can store whatever you want to keep in the warehouse until you're ready to send for it."

"Whatever." Hannah storms off, taking the stairs two at a time as she dashes up to her room. Slamming the door behind her, she collapses on her four-poster bed.

This cheerful room has been her safe haven all her life. Before long, some other little girl will claim it as her own. Will she replace the plush green carpet and cover the yellow walls with pink or purple paint? Hannah's eyes travel the room. What's she supposed to do with all her possessions? She spent twenty-one years accumulating this stuff. Trophies and swim team ribbons. Stuffed animals and her collection of hats. Should she throw it all away? Save any of it for the baby? Does her mother expect Hannah to sell her dollhouse, the one her father made for her, in the yard sale?

Hannah needs to come up with a legitimate plan for her move, so she's not caught off guard the next time Birdie asks about it. Her new job starts in mid-September. Will she stay on Palmetto Island through August and fly out with the baby the week before? When is it safe for a newborn to travel by air? She pulls her phone out of her pocket and googles her question. The consensus is that, as long as mother and baby are healthy, the baby can fly on an airplane as early as two weeks of age. She'll probably connect through Atlanta or Dallas. She envisions herself lugging a baby and luggage through the airport. The plane ride itself will be long. What if the baby screams the whole way? And what will she do when she arrives in San Diego? No one will meet her at the airport. She'll take an Uber to . . . to where? She knows the office address. She'll use Zillow to find a place to rent nearby. But she can't take a baby to an apartment with no furniture. She'll stay in a hotel for a few days until she can buy the basic furniture. She'll sell her Jeep and purchase a new car. There. She has a plan. But all this will cost money. She needs to get a summer job as soon as possible.

Overwhelmed by all the changes and exhausted from her long drive, Hannah closes her eyes and imagines being with her father, their kayaks skimming across the water at dawn. She dozes off and wakes to the sound of her mother calling her to dinner. Rolling off the bed, she goes across the hall to the bathroom where she splashes cold water on her face, combs her fingers through her long hair, and ties it back into a ponytail.

Her mom is waiting for her at the table. Sitting down at her place, Hannah studies the plate of food in front of her—quiche and her favorite salad of baby greens, crispy prosciutto, and honeydew melon. She stopped for lunch in North Carolina, but that was hours ago, and she's suddenly ravished.

Birdie offers the blessing, a responsibility that once belonged to her father, and Hannah forks off a bite of quiche. The filling is rich—crab and eggs and Swiss cheese—and the crust light and flaky. She's eaten her mother's crab quiche before, but this is richer, more flavorful. Birdie, the new baker in town, has upped her game.

But no compliments to Birdie are forthcoming. She's too mad at her mother for selling the house. "When do we have to be out of the house?"

"The yard sale is Saturday. The movers come on Monday."

"Since today is Wednesday, there's no point in me unloading my car. Should I take my stuff to your new apartment?"

Birdie smiles. "I have a load ready to take myself. We'll go tomorrow after lunch, and I'll show you around."

"Okay," Hannah says and finishes her meal in silence.

This is the first time she and Birdie have eaten dinner together since New Year's. Something is missing. Other than her dad. She looks around the room. The Grey Goose bottle is absent from the pine hutch. Her mother is drinking sweet tea instead of vodka. Birdie is on her best behavior for Hannah's first night back.

While doing dishes together afterward, her mother says, "I spoke to Jonathan. He's agreed to extend your health care policy until the end of the year. I'll be getting health care through the bakery once I officially take over the business at the end of the month. Since your insurance with your new job doesn't start until September, I wanted to make certain you're covered when the baby comes."

"Okay. Thanks." Health care insurance is another one of those things Hannah hasn't considered. Until now, her involvement in her insurance has been limited to presenting her card to the receptionist at doctors' appointments. Her heart sinks. When she fills out the forms with her new employer, she must list the baby as a dependent to get health care for him or her. Then everyone in the human resources department at Sandman will know she had a baby over the summer. Word will spread rapidly throughout the firm, and Jeff Brandon will find out. He can't fire her, can he? Surely, there's a law against that kind of discrimination. Even so, she lied to him when she told him she was spending the summer in Europe. A black mark against her before she even has her first day on the job.

After dinner, Birdie brews a cup of chamomile tea and takes it outside to the back porch. The days are longer now, and the sun has begun its descent over the horizon. Sunset views will be even better from her second-floor windows at the new apartment.

She stayed at Max's apartment until a few days ago when she returned home to prepare for the yard sale and move. The lonely memories in this house overshadow the good ones. She never realized how unhappy she was in her marriage. In her life.

Birdie misses her best friend, their long walks, deep talks, and easy companionship. Max has helped her stay sober for eighty-two days, some of them easier than others. Since coming home, she's had to fight to ignore old habits. Countless times, she's found herself standing at the pine hutch, looking for the Grey Goose bottle. Once, she even went as far as to check her old hiding places. But now, with Hannah home, the urge to drink is even worse.

She picks up her phone from the arm of the rocker and clicks on Max's number. Max answers on the second ring. "It's your favorite head case calling for her daily pep talk. Hannah's home. If you come for a visit, bring your hacksaw. You'll need it to cut the tension between us."

Max chuckles. "You expected that, honey. Remember what we talked about."

"Of course. Be patient. Think before I speak. Be a good listener. Don't judge. I've broken all four rules already. I should've told her about selling the house and buying the bakery before she came home."

"You mean you didn't? Oh, Birdie. You have so much to learn. Telling her ahead of time would've given her a chance to adjust. Which would've made her homecoming less awkward."

Tears blur Birdie's vision. "I know, Max. But I was scared Hannah would change her mind about coming home for the summer if she found out she had to live in a two-bedroom apartment with me. I have three months to mend our relationship. If I fail, I may never see her again when she moves out to California."

"Then don't fail."

"As if it were that easy. She's so hostile toward me. And holding my tongue is proving harder than I thought it would be. She has no clue what she's getting herself into. Not only in having a baby and being a single parent but in moving to a faraway strange city where she doesn't know a soul."

"She's moving to San Diego, not Bangkok. FYI, they speak

English in California. She's a likable kid. She'll make friends in no time."

Birdie frowns. "Whose side are you on?"

"Yours," Max says. "And hers. I want what's best for both of you. If she has her heart set on California, you have to let her go."

Birdie sighs. "But she knows so little about the real world. When I told her Jonathan extended her health insurance coverage until the end of the year, she looked at me with a blank face, as though she never considered who would pay the medical bills when the baby comes."

"She's a child having a child. She needs her mama right now."

Birdie blows a strand of hair off her forehead. "And I want to be here for her. I truly do. If only I didn't have my own problems to deal with. Hannah has always looked up to you. Maybe you can get through to her."

"I will certainly try."

"I'm sorry I'm so needy right now."

In a cheerful voice, Max says, "As the saying goes, payback is hell."

"I hope you're never as down and out as I am right now."

"Correction," Max says. "You *were* down and out. You're on the way up, to a brighter future."

"You're the best, Maxie. I don't know what I'd do without you."

Birdie hangs up with Max. As she's getting to her feet, she glimpses movement through the kitchen window. Was that Hannah? Was her daughter eavesdropping on her conversation with Max? Did she overhear Birdie expressing doubt about whether she's prepared for the real world? She and Hannah are definitely not off to a great start.

Birdie doesn't see her daughter again until she emerges from her room with three large boxes around noon the next day. Refusing Birdie's offer of help, Hannah wrestles the boxes down the stairs to the family room. She kicks the box with stuffed animals peeking through the open lid. "This stuff is for the yard sale. The other two go to the warehouse."

Birdie hands Hannah a sheet of stickers. "Price low for quick sale. Whatever money you make, you get to keep."

"How generous of you," Hannah says, snatching the sheet of stickers. "I'll put it toward paying my medical expenses."

Birdie's face falls. So, she *did* overhear her phone conversation with Max.

Hannah peels off a sticker and places it on an old boom box. "What did you do with all Dad's stuff?"

"I burned his clothes. I'm selling the rest."

Hannah's head jerks up. "You burned Dad's clothes. Are you crazy? His suits were custom-tailored."

"If he'd wanted them, he would've taken them with him. It's been four months. He's not coming back, Hannah."

Hannah glares at Birdie. "You don't know that for sure. You can't sell his hunting and fishing equipment. That stuff is worth a fortune. And one of those fishing rods is mine. Wait!" Hannah spins on the heels of her flip-flops and runs to the kitchen window. "Where's the boat? Did you get rid of it, too?"

Birdie joins her at the window. "No, Hannah. I didn't sell the boat. I'm having the bottom painted, and the motor serviced before summer. My new building comes with its own slip at the marina. They even provide racks for kayaks."

"As if that makes up for not having our own dock and our own rack for kayaks."

She angles her body toward Hannah. "I know this is a lot of change at once. But we'll get through it together." When Birdie moves to tuck a lock of Hannah's shiny mahogany hair behind her ear, Hannah slaps her hand away.

Be patient, Birdie warns herself. She steps away from her daughter. "I've already eaten lunch. Why don't you fix yourself a sandwich while I finish loading my car? Then you can follow me over to the apartment. I'll show you the bakery and our boat slip at the marina."

Hannah is grateful for the opportunity to drive herself to the new apartment. It was easier when she was away at school. When she didn't have to see her mom every day. Where she wasn't surrounded by so many memories of her dad.

Hannah overheard her mom on the phone last night. She was no doubt talking to Max, her only friend. Birdie doesn't think Hannah can cut it in the real world, but Hannah intends to prove her wrong. She's only a kid. She has a lot to learn. But she'll figure it out as she goes.

Driving down Ocean Avenue, the main street in their small downtown area, is like traveling back to a time Hannah is too young to remember but has seen in movies. Some businesses have been in the same families for generations. There's Freeman's Hardware with racks of flowering plants displayed out front. And Scoop's Parlor boasting round tables with yellow umbrellas on the sidewalk where customers enjoy double-decker ice cream cones. She passes the women's boutique, new and used bookstore, and a handful of antique shops, some with higher quality merchandise than others.

Hannah longs to continue straight over the causeway to Palmetto Beach, where charming old cottages dot both the ocean and inlet sides of the road. She has fond memories of high school bonfires and surf casting for blues with her father. A vision pops into her head of a little girl and her mom building sandcastles. Is that little girl Hannah? And the mama Birdie? Did they spend days at the beach together when she was a child? Were they ever close? Hannah doesn't remember.

Hannah clears the green light and turns on her blinker. She passes Johnson's Pharmacy—the town's original drug store with an old-fashioned lunch counter— and follows her mother's car down a narrow alley to a small parking lot shared by bakery and pharmacy employees. She joins her mother at the back door, and they enter a small room with wall hooks for coats, a set of built-in wooden lockers, and a staircase leading to the second floor. In the adjacent kitchen, a woman with dark auburn hair secured at the back of her head in a tight bun stands at an enormous mixing bowl.

Birdie calls out to the woman—Sadie is her name—who waves in return.

Hannah trails her mother up the stairs to a large sitting room. She falls immediately in love with the space, the exposed brick wall along one side of the room and natural light spilling in through oversized windows onto worn wooden floors. The room would make an excellent photography studio.

She looks over at her mom who is waiting for her reaction. "You mentioned it was small. You didn't say it was a shoebox." She feels a stab of guilt for intentionally being mean. Why can't she admit the apartment is fab?

Birdie's lips turn down. "Think of it as cozy."

Hannah gestures at a set of cabinets with a sink and under-counter refrigerator. "Is that seriously the kitchen?"

"We have a fully stocked spacial kitchen with commercial appliances downstairs. A kitchenette is all we need up here." Birdie moves over to the brick wall. "I thought we'd put our kitchen table along this wall and arrange the furniture in the living area to take advantage of the view."

"Lovely." With her mother on her heels, Hannah wanders down a short hallway to a large bedroom with the same windows and spectacular light.

"The two bedrooms are identical," Birdie says. "You can have whichever one you want."

"What difference does it make if they're identical?" At the window, Hannah stares out at the boats in the marina. Living above the bakery definitely has perks. She's always loved the boardwalk area with its eclectic mixture of seafood restaurants and bars.

Continuing her tour, she turns her nose up when she sees the bathroom that separates the two bedrooms. "Are you kidding me? We have to share a bathroom?"

Her mother's expression turns icy. "No, Hannah. We don't have to share a bathroom. You're free to rent your own apartment or live with a friend. But this is the best I can offer right now. You are not the only one facing challenges. I quit drinking and—"

"Ha. For how long?"

"I hope forever. But I'm taking it one day at a time. Max is helping and I've started going to AA meetings two nights a week."

"Good luck with that," Hannah says in a doubtful tone. What is wrong with her? She wanted her mom to quit drinking. The problem is, it's too little too late. If her mom had quit drinking sooner, her dad would still be here.

They leave the bedroom and go downstairs. In the kitchen, her mother introduces her to Sadie. "Sadie's been working at the bakery for ten years," Birdie explains. "Bless her soul, she got stuck with the job of training me."

Sadie's smile is warm. "You're doing great, Birdie." She turns to Hannah and studies her. "Aren't you a pretty thing? I see the resemblance."

"Actually, I look like my dad."

"Then he must be a handsome fella," Sadie says, making Hannah feel all the more guilty for acting like a spoiled brat to a woman she's just met. Hannah blames her foul mood on hormones, but she knows it's much more than that. She's made a colossal mistake in coming home for the summer.

Hannah and Birdie leave the kitchen and enter the show-room, standing out of the way of customers waiting at separate service counters for baked goods and coffee. More patrons occupy every table positioned by the windows and at the banquette on the far wall.

"I'm going to close for a few days before Memorial Day to make some minor renovations," Birdie says. "You have such a creative eye, I'd like your thoughts on what improvements we should make. I'm thinking of adding large chalkboard menus behind both counters."

Wait. Did her mom just give her a compliment? Hannah rubs her chin as she thinks about it. "The place has potential, but you need to brighten it up, make it feel more like a cafe. Why not play off the island theme? Put some potted palm trees in the corner and paint the wall behind the counters a fun color like aqua." She tilts her head back, staring up. "Cool, a tin ceiling. I would paint it a paler version of the same hue and replace the brown ceiling fans with white ones. Maybe try to find some that have an islandy feel."

Birdie places her hand on her chest. "Love it! I'll eventually change the name, but we can still use the island theme." She smiles at Hannah. "I knew you'd have creative ideas."

Hannah watches the teenage boy who works alone at the coffee bar. "That poor kid looks overwhelmed. I feel like I should jump in and help him out."

Birdie follows her gaze. "That's Jason. He's a good kid, headed off to college at Auburn in the fall. I'm sure it would thrill him to have some help. The coffee bar manager just quit. She's going back to school to become a chef. I'm hoping you'll consider managing the coffee bar while you're here this summer. I'll pay you a decent salary, and you'll be living rent free. You should be able to save some money for your move to California."

Hannah has to work hard not to let her excitement show. "Sure. Why not? I was planning to get a job, anyway."

Managing the coffee bar will keep her busy. But if she spends as much time on the water as possible and if she avoids her mom as much as possible, maybe she'll survive the summer.

EIGHT

The move goes off without a hitch. Over the course of a few days, Birdie transitions from homeowner to small business owner. She feels no regret about selling her home of twenty-three years. She is ready to move on with her life.

The apartment, with their furniture in place and art on the walls and rugs on the floors, soon feels like home. While Hannah is less hostile than when she first returned from school, she's not the same exuberant girl Birdie remembers from her high school days. Birdie's attempts to make conversation with Hannah are met with silence. Her daughter has a lot on her plate. It's only natural for her to be withdrawn. But Birdie senses there's more to it than that.

"She'll come around," Max says when Birdie expresses her concerns. "These things take time. If it makes you feel any better, I've tried talking to her, and she doesn't have much to say to me either."

"Really? The two of you have always been close."

"Exactly my point," Max says. "She's going through a lot right now. We need to be here for her when she is ready to talk."

Birdie closes the bakery, and mother and daughter spend a

week making improvements. The minor changes have a dramatic impact, and the customers offer praise when they reopen the Friday morning before Memorial Day. They are swamped by long lines of locals and vacationers, stocking up on baked goods for the holiday weekend.

Hannah proves to be an enormous asset at the coffee bar. After working part-time in a coffee shop for two years, she knows her stuff. She suggests a brand change of coffee, and customers rave, as they do about Birdie's new line of tarts, breads, and quiches.

The bakery is open for business every day of the week from nine until six, except on Sundays when they close at two. To celebrate their first successful weekend, Birdie invites Hannah to accompany her for an early dinner at Shaggy's, the Lowcountry-style seafood restaurant next door. Much to Birdie's surprise, Hannah accepts. The weather is ideal, low humidity and sunny skies, and they request a table on the covered porch on the board-walk. When the waitress arrives, without looking at the menus, Hannah and Birdie order steamed shrimp and sweet tea with a basket of hushpuppies to share.

After the waitress leaves, Birdie folds her hands on the table. "So, tell me about your job." She manages a smile, even though the thought of her daughter leaving South Carolina for good makes her feel empty inside.

"My job is with a cyber security firm. They are paying me well."

"That's important. What exactly does a cyber security firm do?"

Hannah looks at Birdie as though she's an idiot. "It's self-explanatory. They protect companies from cyber attacks."

Be patient, Birdie's inner voice warns. "I assumed that. Can you be more specific?"

"I don't wanna talk about it," Hannah snaps.

"You never want to talk about anything these days."

Hannah falls back in her chair. "Because we get along better when we *don't* talk."

The waitress brings over their beverages. Birdie takes a sip, licking her lips at the sweet lemony tea. "I'm trying here, Hannah. I'd like to mend our relationship."

"As if we ever had a relationship to mend." Hannah looks away. "Can we just eat and go home?"

"We can, once the waitress brings our food. Until then, I refuse to sit here in silence." Birdie leans into the table. "Are you taking care of yourself? Have you scheduled an appointment with the obstetrician?"

"I have an appointment for my ultrasound on Tuesday." Hannah's lips curve into a soft smile that transforms her face from a hostile youth to a young woman on the verge of becoming a mother. The smile tells Birdie just how much this baby means to her daughter.

"That's an important appointment. I'd like to go with you, if you'll let me."

"Actually, I was thinking of asking Max to go."

Birdie presses her lips thin. "I'm sure Max would love that."

Hannah stares past Birdie, her eyes narrowing at something or someone behind her. Birdie, who is sitting with her back to the inlet, shifts in her chair to see the object of her daughter's attraction. Hannah's best childhood friend, Liza, sits at a table with a group of boys and girls their age. They are talking and laughing while sipping margaritas.

Birdie feels an ache in her chest for her child. "Oh, honey. I know you'd rather be with them. And you're so young, you *should* be with them, enjoying this phase in your life. Why don't you consider putting the baby up for adoption?"

"For the millionth time, I'm keeping the baby." Hannah moves to the edge of her chair. "I knew this dinner was a bad idea. We can't stand to be in the same room together, let alone at the same table." She stands abruptly, snatching her small shoulder bag off the back of the chair.

As Hannah storms off the porch, Birdie watches Liza's eyes zero in on Hannah's baby bump. Liza's face falls. Does she not know about the baby? Why wouldn't Hannah tell her? Is she embarrassed about not knowing who the father is? As Max is to Birdie, Liza is a tried-and-true friend to Hannah. Their friendship has weathered many storms over the years. But Hannah, having isolated herself from everyone, must feel so alone. If only she would talk to Birdie. If only Birdie would learn to keep her mouth shut. *Think before you speak, Birdie, she tells herself.* She ruined dinner by bringing up adoption, but regardless of Max's rules, Birdie's job as a parent is to make certain her daughter not only understands the sacrifices she's making but that she explores all her options.

With tears blurring her vision, Hannah stares at the ground as she hurries back to the apartment. She doesn't blame Liza for being mad at her, not after the way she blew her off over Christmas. Liza is . . . *was* her best friend. Given the opportunity, Liza would've been sympathetic to Hannah's situation. But Hannah wasn't yet ready to talk about the baby. Now five months have passed. And she has no legitimate excuse for not calling Liza.

Hannah tells herself it doesn't matter. Their lives are on separate courses, anyway. Her friendship with Liza is yet one more thing she's giving up for her unborn child. Flopping down on her bed, she places a hand on her belly, feeling the baby move. She suspected it wouldn't be easy. She never knew it would be this hard.

Hannah's ultrasound appointment is an important milestone she doesn't want to experience alone, and she's grateful when Max agrees to go with her. When she sees her baby on the monitor, all doubts and insecurities vanish. She'll face challenges of epic proportions in raising this baby as a single parent, but the all-consuming love she feels for it will carry her through the worst of times.

"Ten fingers and toes," the ultrasound technician says. "Appears you have a healthy baby. Would you like to know the sex?"

Hannah is tempted, and she looks uncertainly at Max, who raises her hands as if to say don't ask me.

"I can't make that decision for you, sweetheart. I'm all for surprises. On the other hand, knowing the sex enables you to better prepare."

Hannah returns her focus to the monitor. She sees the baby's head and little limbs moving about in their cramped space. Her baby. Her daughter or son. "I'll wait."

Fifteen minutes later, Max and Hannah exit the doctor's office together. "What do you think it is?" Hannah asks.

Max laughs. "Why didn't you find out when you had the chance?"

"Because speculating is more fun."

"I can't argue with that." Max eyes her stomach. "You're carrying it like a boy, but I have a hunch it's a girl. What do *you* think it is?"

"I honestly don't have a feeling one way or another as long as it's healthy."

Max pats her on the back. "Right answer. You're gonna be a good mama."

Hannah walks on air the rest of the way to the car, and stares out the window, lost in thought, during the short ride back to the waterfront. Everything—the morning sickness, hiding the pregnancy, losing friends—has all been worth it. She's receiving the gift of life in return.

"Are you up for ice cream?" Max asks as she navigates her car into the hotel parking lot.

Hannah smiles over at her. "Only if you let me treat you for a change." Max has taken Hannah for ice cream at Scoops to celebrate all her major life events. When she sold the most boxes of Girl Scout cookies. When she landed the leading role in the middle school play. When she got accepted to VCU.

Max parks the car and turns off the engine. "I accept."

They cross the street to the parlor where they order double scoops of butter pecan on sugar cones. When all the tables on the sidewalk are taken, they stroll aimlessly down Ocean Avenue.

Dragging her tongue over her ice cream, Max says, "Wanna talk about your mama? I understand things are tense between the two of you. Giving up the booze has been a real challenge for her. And you're not making things any easier."

Hannah cuts her eyes at Max. "If she'd quit sooner, Dad wouldn't have left."

"You shouldn't be so quick to judge, Hannah. The drinking may have caused problems in their marriage, but Birdie had nothing to do with him embezzling funds from his law firm."

She doesn't respond, because Max is right.

Pausing in front of the wine and cheese shop, Max waves at the owner inside. Hannah nudges her with her elbow. "Why don't you ask Lester out on a date? You know you want to."

Max's face beams red. "Hush up, child, before I take a switch to your behind."

Hannah sticks out an ice cream tongue at her. "I'm all grown up now, Max. You can't spank me anymore."

"Don't test me," she says, her eyes still on Lester Bates. "Maybe I will ask him out. Better do it now while I still have my looks. Certain parts of my body are sagging."

Hannah covers one ear with her free hand. "Ooh. Too much information."

They continue on their way. "I have to hand it to your mama. She hid the drinking well. I never suspected a thing. Was it bad?"

"At times."

They reach the end of the business district and cut over to the boardwalk. Leaning against the railing, they stare out across the inlet as they finish their cones and toss the napkins in a nearby trashcan.

"Mom wanted me to have an abortion, and now she thinks I should give the baby up for adoption. I get that she's disappointed. This certainly isn't how I imagined my life. But I'm trying to make the most of a difficult situation. I need her support right now. Not her criticism."

"Let's sit a spell." Turning away from the railing, Max motions her to a wooden bench. "Your mama only wants what's best for you. Just as you're concerned about your baby, she's concerned about hers. I can't say I blame her for being worried about you, living all the way out on the West Coast alone with no one to help you with the baby."

"But I won't be alone. I'll have Chris."

Max stares at her over the top of her Wayfarer sunglasses. "Oh, really? Who is Chris? Is he a love interest?"

"He has a girlfriend, Max." Hannah laughs at the disappointment that crosses Max's face. "Chris is a good friend from school. The same company that hired me hired him."

"Sounds to me like Chris will be busy with his own life. You'll be adjusting to a new job, trying to make a good impression after being up half the night with a newborn. You'll have to put the baby in daycare, which means the poor little thing will bring home every germ known to man. You'll spend every dime you make paying the pediatrician. And who will take care of you when you get sick?"

Hannah's jaw tightens. "Are you suggesting I give the baby up for adoption?"

"Not at all, sweetheart. I can't imagine letting another woman raise my own flesh and blood. I'm hoping you'll pass on this job and stay closer to home."

"And do what?" Hannah spreads her arms wide. "There's no industry here, other than tourism. I didn't work my butt off in school to become a baker."

Max rests a hand on her shoulder. "But Charleston's just up the road. You could look for a job there. Or in Columbia. Somewhere closer, so your mom and I can get to you in a hurry if you need us."

"You and Mom need to stop worrying so much. I'll be fine."

Hannah gets to her feet, signaling the conversation is over. Max joins her, and they walk back to the bakery in silence. She's always valued Max's opinion, and the dismal image she portrays of Hannah's lonely life with a newborn in California plagues her in the days and weeks ahead.

NINE

Hannah's days fall into a pattern at the bakery. She's out on the water before daybreak, usually in her kayak but sometimes in her father's boat. Her efforts pay off in stunning photographs of the sun rising over the landscape and a host of species of birds coming to life in the dawn of a new day. She creates a business Instagram account and builds a website to showcase her photographs. Although she charges a nominal fee for the most impressive images, she allows most to be downloaded for free. At this stage, her goal isn't to make money but to establish a reputation as a photographer. How her photography hobby will serve her as a cyber security consultant, she hasn't a clue. But the results so far—thousands of followers on Instagram and hundreds of downloads on her website—bode well.

She works at the coffee bar during the day. Business is solid, a constant stream of customers, and Hannah secretly gives her mother credit. The bakery was average before, when Amber owned it. But people have gone nuts over Birdie's baked goods, particularly her key lime pies.

Jason is a sweet kid, even if he's often lazy and comes in most days hungover. Hannah is sometimes envious of him. She'd love to be starting college in the fall instead of a new life that terrifies her.

On a Thursday morning during the third week of June, two of Hannah's high school classmates enter the bakery and make a beeline for the coffee bar. Chloe and Dana belonged to the group of girls Liza and Hannah called The Royals—Chloe being the queen and the others her ladies-in-waiting. They are dressed for the beach with flimsy cover-ups over string bikinis, blonde hair in ponytails, and designer sunglasses propped on heads.

Because Jason is busy with other customers, Hannah has the privilege of waiting on them.

"Hannah, how lovely to see you. Are you working here now? And to think of all the money your parents wasted on your college education. How are your parents, by the way?" Chloe brings her manicured fingers to her lips. "Oops. Sorry. Didn't mean to bring up a touchy subject. I forgot about your father's mysterious disappearance."

Hannah flashes Chloe her brightest smile. "I'm sure your snarky sense of humor made you popular with the sorority bitches at Chapel Hill."

Chloe examines her manicured fingernails. "I was president of said sorority, actually."

"Good for you." Hannah pours two black coffees and slides them across the counter to Chloe and Dana.

Chloe takes her coffee. "You know, Hannah, I learned to drink my coffee black when I discovered intermittent fasting. I'm back to my high school cheerleading weight. You should try it. You could stand to lose a few."

"If I cared about dieting, Chloe, I wouldn't be working in a bakery." She processes their charges and hands them back their debit cards. Swallowing the lump in her throat, she moves on to the next person in line.

While she works, out of the corner of her eye, she watches Chloe and Dana, sitting side-by-side on the banquette. She's acutely aware of the sound of their giggles as they look back and forth between their phones and Hannah. She tells herself she doesn't care. But she totally does.

They stay at the table long after they've finished their coffees, taking up space while other customers wait to sit down. When they finally get up to leave, they saunter past the coffee bar on their way out. "Bye bye, Hannah," they say in sugary sweet tones, rotating their cupped hands like beauty queens in a parade.

Later that night, while lying in bed, Hannah scrolls through her Instagram feed, feeling lonelier than ever at the sight of her friends enjoying their lives and exploring the world. Her breath hitches when she clicks on Chloe's story and sees a pic of herself with an arrow pointed to her protruding belly, which is no longer a bump but a mound. Hannah's head is cut off, and bold text flashes across the bottom of the image. *Can you guess who this is?*

Anger burns deep inside Hannah. But fear is there as well. She clicks on Chloe's profile and scrolls through her list of followers. Hannah knows the local kids, but there are hundreds of others. How many of her friends from Chapel Hill have connections to people from Columbia? People who might know Ryan.

Hannah longs to talk to Chris. She misses him like crazy. But his parents don't have internet or cell service on their farm in China. She considers calling Liza. She despises The Royals as much as Hannah. At almost eleven o'clock, she's no doubt out with her friends at a bar or party, enjoying this phase in life Hannah's mom is so obsessed with.

For the first time in a long time, Hannah cries herself to sleep.

Chloe and Dana return late morning on Friday, wearing shorts and T-shirts with bikini straps tied behind necks and smug grins on faces. Hannah glances around. Only two other customers are in the bakery, eating a late breakfast at a table by the window. Today is Jason's day off, and Sadie and Birdie are in the back.

"Get your cameras ready, girls," Hannah says, and lifts her white bakery polo up to reveal her swollen belly.

Chloe's and Dana's mouths fall open.

"That's right. I have nothing to hide. I'm pregnant. The baby is due in early August."

Chloe covers her eyes with the back of her hand. "That's just gross, Hannah. Please lower your shirt. As if we care whether or not you're pregnant."

Hannah pulls her shirt down. "You cared enough yesterday to post a pic of me in your story."

"I have no idea what you're talking about." She fishes her wallet out of her canvas beach bag. "Please, I need coffee. You missed a great party last night on the beach. Poor you. I guess you've been missing a lot of those lately. Not much fun to go to a party when you can't drink."

"I'm pregnant, Chloe, not contagious with some deadly virus. I could go out if I wanted. But I have plenty to keep me busy."

Chloe rolls her eyes. "Yeah, right?"

Chloe and Dana pay for their coffees and take them over to the banquette. Once again, Hannah can feel them watching her. And once again, she finds a pic of her baby bump on Chloe's Instagram story that night. And hence, begins a pattern that takes place over the next ten days.

Terrified Ryan will show up and stake his claim on his unborn child, Hannah keeps one eye on the bakery's front door at all times. She's certain that, by now, one of their mutual friends has seen Chloe's pics and put two and two together. Maybe Ryan doesn't care. Maybe he doesn't want to be a part of his child's life. Maybe he's not interested in wrecking his future as a lawyer. The anxiety of not knowing makes her a nervous wreck. She has trouble sleeping at night, and she snaps at everyone around her. Even her photography suffers. She can hardly wait to move to California. The idea of being twenty-five hundred miles away from Ryan and Chloe gets her through the agonizing days. Then, out of the blue, her prayers are answered when Chloe leaves to spend the Fourth of July week with her family on Sullivan's Island.

———

Every day Birdie remains sober is a blessing. One minute, she's on top of the world. And the next minute she feels like she's teetering on the edge of a cliff.

"Am I doing something wrong?" she asks Max. "I feel like it's getting harder and harder to stay away from the booze."

Max embraces her. "You're just stressed out about Hannah. But you're doing great. Hang in there."

Birdie pulls away from her friend. "I'm not making any progress with Hannah. And it's not just me. She's testy with everyone these days, including Sadie and Jason."

And more than once, Birdie hears Hannah speak to their customers in an irritable tone of voice. After one such incident, when the disgruntled customer stomps off in a huff, Birdie confronts her about it. "You're nearing the end of your pregnancy, Hannah. You're uncomfortable and understandably grumpy. But you can't take it out on the customers."

Hannah's shoulders slump. "I know, and I'm sorry. I'll try harder."

"Can I do anything for you? Or get you anything?"

Hannah looks up, the hint of a smile on her lips. "I'm craving donuts. Will you make one for me?"

Birdie shakes her head, as though she misheard her daughter. "A donut?"

"Yes, a donut. There's this awesome donut shop in Richmond. We used to go there all the time after class."

"I'm sorry to say I know nothing about making donuts. But we have a fryer. If you want to make this your project, I'm happy to help."

Leaning back against the counter, arms folded over chest, Hannah stares up at the ceiling. "Hm. Maybe I will. How hard can it be?"

Birdie envisions them working together to develop a whole new line of donut products, but the next afternoon, she enters the kitchen to find Sadie and Hannah with their heads pressed together over a hissing fryer.

"What're y'all making?"

"Blueberry cake donuts," Hannah says, her eyes on the sizzling dough.

"Your daughter inherited your talent for baking." A wide grin spreads across Sadie's face as she rubs her stomach. "I got to sample the first batch, and I'm here to tell you, they are some kinda good. Wait until you try one."

Birdie watches her daughter remove three dozen donuts from the fryer and drizzle glaze over the top of each. When they're cool enough to eat, she picks one up and takes a bite. Her blue eyes grow wide. "These are delicious," she says in mid chew. "The customers will love them."

Hannah offers her a rare smile. "We made yeast donuts, too, in honor of the Fourth of July." She gestures at a nearby tray of donuts decorated in red, white, and blue icing.

Birdie studies the donuts. "Patriotic donuts. How adorable. These will be a hot seller. If this is all you have, you better make more."

Hannah nods. "I'm already on it. I have ideas for other flavors, too."

Birdie loads the blueberry donuts on a tray and places it alongside the patriotic donuts on the top shelf of the showcase. The donuts sell out within an hour. "You just got yourself a raise," she says to her daughter. "Keep up the outstanding work."

Birdie gives her daughter free rein to experiment, and Hannah implements the daily donut special, offering seasonal flavors like peach cobbler, strawberry shortcake, and banana pudding. While making donuts goes a long way toward improving Hannah's overall temperament, she's still irritable at times. The following week, Birdie watches her daughter closely for clues. By the end of the week, she identifies two of the more popular girls from her high school class as the source of her daughter's ill humor. Chloe and Dana come into the bakery every day dressed for the beach in bathing suits and coverups. Does Hannah regret missing out on the fun? Is she finally realizing what she'll be sacrificing by having this baby at such a young age?

As she watches and listens from a far, Birdie overhears the girls talking about Instagram. Pulling out her phone, she accesses the Island Bakery Instagram account. She took the account over from Amber. The account has thousands of followers, and Amber followed many of them back. One of them being Chloe. She clicks on Chloe's profile and sees at least a dozen photographs of a young pregnant woman. Although her head is cut off in all the images, Birdie recognizes her daughter. The top left image offers a side view of Hannah's belly, which takes up most of the real estate in the picture. The text beneath the photograph reads: *Place your bets now.* The link provided takes Birdie to an online polling website where hundreds of people have speculated about who the mother is and the length, weight, sex, and due date of the baby.

Why would Chloe do such a thing? The girls were never friends in high school, but this is downright cruel.

Birdie's blood boil, and the phone shakes in Birdie's hand. She needs a drink. She grabs her purse and heads out the back door. But when she reaches her car, a voice inside her head warns, "Don't do it."

She marches down the alley and across the small park to the Island Hotel, where she finds Max alone at the front desk. "You won't believe this." She shoves her phone in Max's face.

Max takes the phone from her. "What on earth? Is that what I think it is?"

"Yep. My daughter's pregnant stomach." Birdie jabs her finger at the phone. "This is why Hannah's been so down lately." Her face flushes. "I'm so angry I could scream."

"Don't. Please. I have a house full of guests." Max studies the photos more closely. "Hannah's head is cut off in every picture. There's no way anyone can identify her."

"But Hannah knows it's her. Chloe is cyber bullying her. And the stress is taking its toll. It's not good for the baby."

Max looks up from the phone. "Or for you. Do you need to go to a meeting?"

She snatches back the phone and stares at Chloe's smug mug. "Yes, but not until I teach this little girl a proper lesson."

Max eyes her suspiciously. "And how do you plan to do that?"

"With your help. You know practically everyone in both Carolinas and Georgia. Find me some dirt on Chloe Taylor."

Max pauses as she thinks about it. "Actually, I do know a family whose child went to Chapel Hill with Chloe." Drawing a stool up to her computer, her fingers fly across the keyboard as she accesses her client data base.

Birdie goes around behind the counter and stares over Max's shoulder at the computer screen.

"This family is from Greenville. The Parkers. Their daughter, Abigail, is a sweet girl." Max reaches for her phone. "She left her favorite bikini here during their stay. I may have her number from when she texted me about it." She scrolls through her contacts. "Yep. Here it is. I'll be right back."

Max clicks on the number, jumps off the stool, and takes her call to the adjacent lounge. Birdie stands in the doorway watching Max, with phone pressed to ear, pace back and forth in front of the bar. Although she can't hear the conversation, Max's brows are pinched together in concern. Whatever Abigail is telling Max is serious business.

Max ends the call and returns to the lobby.

"Well?" Birdie says.

"Let's go for a walk. I can't afford for any of my guests to overhear me gossiping." Max puts her *Be Right Back* sign on the desk, and taking Birdie by the hand, leads her outside.

Instead of going left past the park to the bakery, Max heads right toward the residential section of old Victorian-style cottages.

"You're killing me, Max. Tell me what you found out about Chloe."

Max stops walking and turns to face Birdie. "Her sophomore year in college, Chloe got messed up at a fraternity party one night. Abigail thinks she might have been on drugs. She got sick in the girl's bathroom and threw up all over her clothes. She came out of the bathroom naked, and a bunch of kids videotaped her with their phones. Needless to say, the story went viral."

"How dare Chloe bully Hannah after what happened to her." Birdie turns away from Max and race-walks back toward the bakery.

Max jobs to catch up with her. "What are you going to do?"

"I'm not sure yet. I'll figure out something."

"I promised Abigail I wouldn't reveal my source."

Continuing on at a fast pace, Birdie glances sideways at her. "No worries. I promise I won't tell anyone where I heard this."

The old friends part in front of the hotel. Birdie goes around to the bakery's back door and hurries up the stairs to her computer. After searching the internet for an hour, she finds the video deep within the recesses of YouTube. Chloe, naked as a jaybird, stumbling around stoned out of her mind.

Birdie bookmarks the video on her phone, and after a night spent tossing and turning in anger, she's waiting for them when Chloe and Dana enter the bakery the following morning.

Hannah has already taken their order when Birdie emerges from the kitchen. "Morning, girls."

Chloe flips her blonde hair over her shoulder. "Morning, Mrs. . . . um . . . What am I supposed to call you now that your husband has left you?"

Any hesitancy Birdie has about her plan vanishes. "I don't want you to call me anything, Chloe. I want you to stop cyber bullying my daughter."

"I don't know what you're talking about?"

"Yes, you do. And if you don't stop immediately, I'll be forced to share this little video I found of you. Coincidentally, did you know the bakery has over ten thousand followers? One of them is your mama." Birdie clicks play on the video and holds the screen out to Chloe.

The color drains from her face and sparks of anger flash in her blue eyes. "Where'd you get that?"

"Interesting thing about social media—pictures and posts never really go away. They can come back to haunt you at the most inconvenient times."

Dana steps away from Chloe, distancing herself from her best friend as though she didn't previously know about the video. Which is not surprising, since she went to a different college from Chloe. And it's not something someone would brag about.

"Let me see that." Hannah snatches the phone from Birdie. She gawks at the video. "Jeez, Chloe, what mind-altering drug were you on that night? And what happened to your clothes?"

Birdie answers for Chloe. "She puked all over them in the girl's bathroom."

Through gritted teeth, Chloe says, "Put. The phone. Away. I will stop posting photographs of Hannah. I was getting bored with it, anyway."

"You'll also take down the poll and trash the results."

"Fine. Let's get outta here." Leaving their coffees on the counter, Chloe grabs Dana by the elbow and drags her toward the door.

"And girls," Birdie calls after them. "Find yourselves another coffee shop. You're no longer welcome here."

After watching them go, Hannah turns to Birdie, offering her a high five. "Mom! That was so badass. I can't believe you just did that." Hannah throws her arms around Birdie's neck, and for several wonderful seconds, Birdie feels the warmth of her daughter's body against hers. This human connection with her own flesh and blood is the key to her happiness. Forget the booze. This is her new drug. And she must get more of it.

TEN

The Chloe situation earns Birdie brownie points with her daughter, and as the morning progresses, she brainstorms ways to take advantage of being in her daughter's good graces. The idea comes to her as she's serving a young mother and her little girl, who smell of sunscreen and wear bathing suits under cover-ups. The beach was Hannah's and Birdie's favorite place when Hannah was a young child.

"What say you and I spend the afternoon at the beach?" she suggests to Hannah during a lull in business. "We can go now and let Sadie and Jason close up."

Hannah's face lights up, and then she drops her smile. "I don't know, Mom. I'm so big. And I don't have a bathing suit."

"Then wear shorts. We'll dig our toes in the sand, maybe go for a walk. And we can pick up sandwiches from the Sandwich Shack for a picnic. We've been working so hard. It'll do us good to get some fresh air."

Hannah shrugs. "Sure. Why not? I haven't been to the beach all summer."

Birdie tries to remember the last time she went to the beach.

It's been years. Maybe even a decade. Which is pathetic considering she lives just a few miles away.

Not much conversation passes between mother and daughter during the afternoon, but instead of being awkward, the silence, for once, is comfortable. After eating turkey and ham club sandwiches for lunch, they read for a while—Birdie her current romance novel and Hannah a pregnancy book— before taking a long walk down the beach.

They stay on the beach until late afternoon and return home tired and sunburned despite being diligent about applying sunscreen. The air conditioner feels cool against their warm skin, and they plop down on either end of the sofa in the living room.

"Thanks for suggesting the beach, Mom. I really needed that."

Birdie smiles at her daughter. "Does this mean we're friends again?"

"Mom . . . I . . ." Hannah averts her eyes, staring out the window. "One afternoon at the beach doesn't change anything."

Sitting up, Birdie swings her legs over the side of the sofa. "What's it gonna take, Hannah? I'm desperate to mend our relationship."

"How desperate? Are you ready to accept the fact that I'm keeping the baby?"

Birdie pauses before answering. "I will always be here for you when you need me. But I don't approve of you keeping the baby. I think you're ruining your life."

Hannah rolls her ample body off the sofa to her feet. "Is that what you did when you had me? Ruin your life? You quit your nursing job because of me. Am I the reason you became a drunk? Your life has been so miserable because of me."

Birdie jumps up. "Hannah, no! That's not true at all."

"I don't believe you," Hannah screams. "If it wasn't me, then what was it? Was it Dad? Was he the reason you started drinking?"

Birdie opens her mouth to speak and closes it again. The answer isn't a simple one.

"So, it *was* me." Grabbing her bag off the dining table, Hannah tears down the stairs, slamming the door behind her on her way out.

Birdie should go after her, but her body is paralyzed, her feet glued to the floor. She's so tired of the drama. The constant worry. The relentless urge to drink. Phone in hand, she moves to the window. She's scrolling down her favorites list for Max's number when Max emerges from the hotel lobby. Pocketing her phone, she watches Max greet their friends, Kelly and Bonnie, on the boardwalk and disappear under the covered porch at Shaggy's.

Birdie feels a pang of envy that they didn't invite her to join them. She needs a drink. She's been sober for 156 days. She's no longer an alcoholic. One vodka tonic won't kill her. She glances at her watch. Ten minutes until the liquor store closes. She hurries out to the car and speeds through town, making it just in time to purchase a handle of vodka.

Back at home, she forgoes the tonic—she doesn't have any, anyway—and fills a lowball glass with ice and vodka. She hides the handle in the cabinet under the sink. She doesn't want Hannah to see it when she comes home. She takes her drink to the window and sips vodka while observing the boats coming and going at the marina below.

The vodka goes down way too smoothly, and a sense of calm overcomes her. She pours another.

She replays her conversation with Hannah. She broke two of Max's rules. She didn't think before she asked Hannah if they were friends again. What kind of stupid question is that? They've never been friends. And Birdie judged Hannah when she accused her of ruining her life. Why did Birdie say that? Because, despite her many flaws, she's not a liar.

What was it Hannah said? *Did I ruin your life? You quit your nursing job because of me.*

True, Birdie willingly gave up nursing to stay at home with her daughter. But Hannah didn't ruin her life. Hannah *is* her life. And now she's gone. But where did she go? She wouldn't have gone to Liza's, since they're no longer friends. Maybe she drove back over to the beach. Or maybe she went for takeout. Birdie tries calling Hannah, but the call goes immediately to voice mail. She tries again and again and again. Ten times in all. But her daughter doesn't pick up. She was angry when she left. Please, God, don't let her get in an accident.

Am I the reason you became a drunk? A drunk. She's been sober for 156 days and her daughter still thinks of her as a drunk. If it looks like a duck, it probably is a duck. She drains the vodka and refills her glass.

Does this mean we're friends again? When were Hannah and her mom ever friends?

With no particular destination in mind, Hannah gets on the highway headed toward Charleston. She rolls her window down, letting the wind whip her hair around her face, as she crosses over the marsh. She turns the radio volume up. Jimmy Buffet is singing "Grapefruit-Juicy Fruit." The song reminds her of her father—it was one of his favorites—and she bursts into tears. The irony of the words makes her cry harder. Her father left her at home alone and crying.

By the time she gets ahold of herself, she's driven around Charleston and is on the interstate going to Columbia. She ignores her mother's calls. She can't talk to Birdie right now. The day had gone so well. Hannah smiles when she thinks about the way Birdie handled Chloe. She didn't know her mom possessed that kind of spunk.

A hundred miles later, on the outskirts of Columbia, Hannah stops for gas and remains at the pump long after the tank is full.

Why did she end up in Columbia? Did she come here to see Ryan? She's eight months pregnant. She can't just show up at his parents' door. What does she want from him? Marriage? No. She thought she loved him once, but she hardly thinks of him anymore. Is she looking for help with the baby? No way. She's not sharing custody of her baby.

The driver of a pickup truck blasts his horn at her, and she moves her car to a marked parking space in front of the convenience store. She has to pee, but the customers inside look shady. She puts the car in reverse and gets back on the highway, headed in the opposite direction toward home.

Her mind is clearer on the drive back to Palmetto Island, and she's able to face a few realities. One. She's not at all excited about a career in cyber security. Two. She loves computers, but she needs to express her creativity. Three. Aside for the baby growing inside of her, photography and tinkering on her website are the only things making her happy right now. Four. California seems like a million miles away, and she doesn't want to leave Palmetto Island, but she can't continue living with Birdie.

By the time she arrives home, her bladder is about to burst, and she hurries inside. At the top of the stairs, she stops short at the sight of her mother passed out on the floor. Fear grips her and pee flows down her legs. She drops to her knees beside Birdie, but she's scared to touch her body. There's a broken glass on the floor. Careful to avoid the jagged pieces, she drags her fingertip through the clear liquid and brings it to her tongue. Vodka.

She lets out a scream that curdles her own blood. This is all Hannah's fault. She drove her mom to drink after months of sobriety.

Hannah calls Max. "Max! Come quick! I think Mama is dead."

"Call 9-1-1. I'm on my way."

With shaking hands, Hannah punches in the numbers. "My mom is passed out on the floor," she tells the emergency operator.

"Is she breathing?" the operator asks.

"I don't know," Hannah screams. "Send an ambulance! Please!"

"I know you're upset, honey, but try to get ahold of yourself."

Max appears at her side. Taking the phone from Hannah, she says, "Go clean yourself up, honey, while I talk to the operator."

It takes Hannah a minute to realize she's talking about her soaked shorts. She does as she's told, quickly changing into dry shorts.

When she returns to the living room, she stands away from her mom, afraid to get too near. Max looks up at Hannah. "The ambulance is on the way. They'll be here momentarily. She's going to be okay, Hannah. She just had too much to drink. Can you tell me what happened?"

"We had a fight." Hannah brings a trembling hand to her mouth. "I said some really mean things to her, Max."

"People have arguments, Hannah. That's part of life. You didn't drive her to drink. Your mama's disease got the best of her."

Disease. This is the first time Hannah has thought of her mother's drinking as a disease. Something she can't control. Something Hannah isn't responsible for. Hannah turns her back on her mother. She can't stand to see her mother so still, so lifeless. What if she isn't okay? What if she dies? She's already lost her father. She's too young to lose both her parents. She needs her mother. What does Hannah know about taking care of a baby?

There's a pounding on the door downstairs, and Max hollers, "Come in! We're up here."

A pair of first responders, a male and female, wrestle a gurney up the stairs. To Hannah's surprise, Liza, wearing the same navy-blue uniform, brings up the rear.

She hurries over to Hannah. "Are you okay? Is the baby okay?"

Hannah hugs her belly. "We're fine. Why are you here?"

"I work for the rescue squad now," Liza says. "Long story."

The other female crew member—Mary, according to her nameplate—cranes her neck to see Hannah. "How much did she drink?"

Hannah shrugs. "I don't know. I've been gone all night. I came home and found her like this." She spots a handle of vodka on the kitchen counter. Only a third of the vodka remains. She gestures at the handle. "She actually quit drinking months ago. She must have bought that tonight after I left."

"Any other addictions? Opioids? Cocaine or meth?" the male paramedic, Paul, asks.

Hannah shakes her head. "No!"

"Let's get her to the hospital," he says to Mary, and they lift Birdie onto their gurney.

Liza turns to Hannah. "Do you want to ride with us in the ambulance?"

Hannah casts a doubtful glance at Max, who says, "Go ahead, sweetheart. I'll meet you at the hospital."

Hannah follows Liza outside. While Mary and Paul load her mother into the back of the ambulance, Liza helps Hannah into the front passenger seat. "I'm gonna ride in the back with your mama. I'll see you at the hospital," she says and closes the door.

Mary climbs behind the wheel, and they speed through the quiet Sunday night streets of Palmetto Island to the hospital on the outskirts of town. Inside the emergency room, Mary and Paul whisk her mother off down the hall. When Hannah starts to go with them, Liza holds her back.

"Give them a few minutes. The doctor will come out to talk to you after he's examined your mom." Liza leads Hannah over to a row of uncomfortable chairs.

Hannah grips her purse to her chest. "Will Mom be okay?"

"I think so. Her pulse is strong. And she was semiconscious on the way over."

Hannah relaxes back in her chair. "When did you become an EMT?"

"At the beginning of the summer. I'm taking the MCAT in August and applying to medical schools in the fall. I wanted to tell you over Christmas, but . . ."

"I blew you off. I'm sorry, Liza. I'd just found out I was pregnant, and I wasn't ready to talk about it."

"What about all the months since then?" Liza asks, her expression tight. "We've been best friends since forever, Han."

Tears blur Hannah's vision. "My dad's disappearance messed me up. I was crazy busy this spring, applying for jobs and trying to keep my pregnancy hidden." She chokes back a sob. "Those are lame excuses. The truth is, I was afraid you would be disappointed in me. That you would no longer want to be my friend."

"As if that could ever happen." Liza puts an arm around Hannah's shoulders and pulls her close. "I love you, silly. We're best friends forever—"

"Through thick and thin," Hannah says, finishing their motto.

Liza gives her a squeeze before removing her arm from her shoulders. "Is the baby Ryan's?"

Hannah rubs her stomach. "This baby is mine, Liza."

Max arrives, saving Hannah from further interrogation. Before Max can sit down, a young doctor approaches them. "Are you here for Bernadette Fuller?"

Hannah jumps to her feet. "We are! How is she?"

"She's going to be fine. She'll be able to go home in a couple of hours."

"Can I see her?" Hannah asks. "I'm her daughter."

"Not yet. We're pumping her stomach and giving her some fluids."

"Will you tell her I'm here? And that her best friend, Max, is with me?"

He nods. "Of course." Turning his back on them, he moves over to the nearby nurses' station.

Liza's unit is summoned for another call. "I've gotta run," she

94

says. "If I don't come back before you leave, I'll check in with you later."

Max and Hannah sit down together. "Do you want to talk about it?" Max asks.

"It happened so fast, Max. Mom and I had a nice day at the beach together, and then boom, we got into a fight. She told me she doesn't approve of me keeping the baby, and she thinks I'm ruining my life. I said some things I shouldn't have, and then I left. I got in my car, and the next thing I knew, I was in Columbia. After stopping for gas, I turned around and came home. When I got back, I found Mom passed out on the floor."

Max shakes her head in pity. "Poor Birdie. I thought she was doing better."

"I'm the problem, Max. She hates me."

"Hush up, child. That's nonsense, and you know it." Max takes hold of Hannah's hand, and they sit in silence for the next thirty minutes until Liza returns from her call.

"That was fast," Hannah says.

"Heart attack patient. The guy lives nearby. We got him here in a hurry. Any word about your mom?"

"Not yet."

Within minutes, an attractive nurse appears. "She's asking for Max."

"But what about me?" Hannah thumbs her chest. "I'm her daughter."

"I'm sorry, hon. Only one person is allowed with her at a time."

Liza places an arm around her shoulders. "Come on, Hannah. We'll take you home."

"Hannah called me a drunk," Birdie says when Max enters her examination cubicle.

"And so you overdose on alcohol to prove she's right?" Max lowers herself to the edge of the bed. "You haven't listened to anything I've been saying to you over these past few months. You broke all the rules."

"She asked me a question, and I told her the truth. I *do* think she's ruining her life. What was I supposed to say?"

"That you're proud of her for choosing the difficult path."

Which is also the truth. Despite everything, she is proud of Hannah for not taking the easy way out. Birdie sucks at relationships. She deserves to be alone. Tears spill from her eyelids. "I'm a failure. I've run my husband away and destroyed my relationship with my daughter."

"You have destroyed nothing. You still have time. Hannah loves you, Birdie. You should've seen her tonight. You scared the daylights out of her. Poor thing wet her pants when she found you lying unconscious on the floor. Why'd you do it, Birdie? Why did you resort to drinking? Why didn't you call me?"

Birdie looks away. "I was calling you when I saw you entering Shaggy's with Kelly and Bonnie. It hurt my feelings you didn't ask me to go with you."

Max lets out a sigh. "Your big birthday's coming up. Turning fifty is a big deal. We were planning a surprise for you. We were thinking about a girls' getaway, maybe an overnight trip to Charleston."

"Oh," Birdie says, feeling like a fool.

The nurse brings Birdie's release papers, and the old friends ride back to the waterfront in silence. At the bakery, Max offers to come in and help her get settled, but Birdie says, "I'm fine. I just need some sleep."

Upstairs in the apartment, Hannah's door is closed, but Birdie hears muffled sobs from within. Birdie's responsible for everything that happened tonight. She upset her daughter and scared her so badly she peed in her pants.

Birdie enters her bedroom, but she doesn't turn on the light.

Outside her window, a full moon shines bright on the inlet, the rippling salty water. Thinking back on her recurrent dream from a few months ago, she imagines diving into the murky water, and when her lungs run out of oxygen, sinking to the muddy bottom of the creek. She bounced back after hitting rock bottom in February. She stayed sober 156 days. But this bottom is different. The anguish she experienced then doesn't touch what's she's feeling now. This is quicksand, gripping her tight, pulling her down and sucking the life out of her one fraction of an inch at a time.

ELEVEN

Nine o'clock rolls around early on Monday morning. Sadie and Hannah open the bakery without Birdie, but when lunchtime comes and goes, Hannah knocks lightly on Birdie's door. "Mom, can I get you anything?"

Birdie doesn't answer.

Hannah tries the knob, but it's locked.

"Are you okay?"

"I'm fine," her mother says in a weak voice. "I'm taking a sick day."

A sick day? The cocktail flu? Since when does a hangover qualify as a sick day? "What about the bakery?"

"You and Sadie can handle it."

This infuriates Hannah, and she steps away from the door. She didn't buy this business. The bakery isn't her responsibility.

Hannah and Sadie hold things together without her. Although more than one customer expresses their disappointment in not being able to buy one of Birdie's key lime pies.

"Why don't we make the pies?" Hannah says to Sadie. "Where's the recipe?"

Sadie taps her forehead. "In your mama's head."

"Then we need to come up with something to replace the pies."

"Why go to the trouble when Miss Birdie will be back tomorrow?"

"I guess you're right." Hannah doesn't tell Sadie about her mom's trip to the hospital on Sunday night. There's no reason for her to know her employer is an alcoholic. But, as the days go by with no sign of Birdie, Sadie's concern mounts. "Maybe Miss Birdie should see a doctor."

"She's fine, Sadie. She's just dealing with some emotional stuff. You know my dad left her, right?"

"Mm-hmm. I heard something about that. Well, until Birdie is back on her feet, why don't we replace the key limes pies with peach cobbler? My granny's recipe is the best. And this summer's crop of South Carolina peaches is particularly flavorful and juicy."

"Sounds good to me."

With double homemade crusts, the cobblers are more time-consuming to make and therefore demand a higher price. But the pies fly out the door, and Sadie can't make them fast enough.

On Thursday morning, Jason doesn't show up for work, and he texts Hannah that he's not coming back. Hannah knocks on Birdie's door. "Jason quit, Mom, without giving notice. What should I do?"

"Hire someone else," her mother says from within.

Hannah places a *Help Wanted* sign in the window, and on Friday, she hires a local woman in her late twenties. Amanda, a self-starter, is more than qualified to take over management of the coffee bar for Hannah when the time comes.

Max checks in daily, and Liza stops by for visits most after-noons. When business is slow, they sip sweet tea at a table by the window and talk for hours about their futures. Liza plans to continue with the rescue squad until she goes to medical school.

She'll make an excellent emergency room doctor. She's the smartest person Hannah knows.

"After medical school, I plan to make Palmetto Island my permanent home," Liza says.

"Why? Wouldn't you make more money in a big city hospital?"

"Money isn't everything, Han. I love being on the coast. Salt water runs through my veins."

"But we know all the guys here. None of them are marriage material." Not that Liza will have any trouble finding a man when she's ready. She's gorgeous with thick auburn hair and emerald-green eyes and a killer body.

"I've got it all figured out. I'm going to meet my guy in medical school. If he loves me, he'll move here to Palmetto Island. If he refuses, I'll find someone else or become a spinster."

Hannah laughs. She wishes she could be so practical about matters of the heart.

In her spare time, Hannah designs a website and advertises her services as a web designer on social media. She uses some of her photography money to purchase a desktop computer, and on Sunday afternoon, she enlists Sadie's teenage boys' help in bringing her old desk over from the warehouse. While combing through the contents of the warehouse, she discovers a white wooden crib, which she assumes was hers when she was a baby. Birdie never mentioned the crib. Another sign she doesn't want Hannah and the baby to stay on in Palmetto Island.

Hannah also finds two boxes of baby things—soft jersey crib sheets, blankets, and hooded towels. She moves the boxes, along with the crib, to the apartment. She sets the desk up in front of the window and the crib on the wall near her bed. The room is large, and even with the extra furniture, there is plenty of space to move around.

When Hannah receives no inquiries about her web design

business, she realizes she needs to showcase her talents and spends every free moment of the following week creating a flashy website for the bakery. She's at her desk, putting the last touches on the site on Sunday afternoon, when Liza comes bounding up the stairs.

"Come with me. I have a surprise for you." Taking her hand, Liza pulls her to her feet and leads her down the stairs and through the kitchen. A group of women in the café yell, "Surprise!"

Sadie and Max are here, along with a small group of Hannah's and Liza's closest classmates and their mothers. Pink and blue balloons float about the room, and tables are arranged into groupings for refreshments, games, and gifts.

Hannah is moved to tears. She turns to Liza. "I can't believe you did this for me."

Liza beams. "You're having a baby, Hannah. These moments in life should be celebrated, even if they happen ahead of schedule."

As the group surrounds her, embracing her and offering congratulations, out of the corner of her eye, Hannah spots Max sneaking away into the kitchen.

"I heard you got a job in California," Mattie says. "That is *so* cool."

Hannah smiles at Mattie. She was the party girl in their group. Never very studious, but always fun to hang out with.

"In cyber security," Liza says in a bragging tone. "She designs websites on the side. She's very talented."

"Oh, really?" says Miss Allison, Mattie's mother and the town's florist. "My website is long overdue an overhaul."

"Me too!" Miss Jenny, another mother and romance author, pipes in. "I need a website to showcase my novels. I've been putting it off for years. I know nothing about managing a website."

"Do you have a business card?" Miss Allison asks.

"Not yet," Hannah says, mentally adding business cards to her growing to-do list. "But I can give you my contact info."

Liza grabs a notepad off the coffee bar and scribbles Hannah's cell number on two sheets of paper, handing one to each of the mothers.

Hannah beams. "If you'd like to see an example of my work, check out the website I built for the bakery at islandbakery.com."

Loud knocking on the door wakes Birdie from a deep sleep. Disoriented, she sits up in bed, raking her fingers through her greasy hair.

"Open this door, Birdie, or I'm calling the fire department to come beat it down."

"Go away, Max."

"I'm unlocking my phone. I'm punching in a nine and a one and another—"

Birdie stumbles to the door and flings it open. "What's your problem? I'm taking a nap."

"Ha. Longest nap in the history of naps. You've been hiding out up here for two weeks now."

Still gripping the doorknob, Birdie says, "Exactly. My bedroom is my safe haven. There's no booze to tempt me, and I can't insult Hannah with the many callous words that find their way to my lips."

Max brushes past her. "That's it. Your little pity party is officially over. Your very pregnant daughter has been working overtime to compensate for your absence. She's been standing on her swollen feet all day while you've been up here feeling sorry for yourself." She jabs her finger at the floor. "Her friends are downstairs, throwing her a surprise baby shower as we speak. You're gonna get yourself cleaned up, which includes taking a shower and putting on a nice sundress, and then go to that party like a proud grandmama-to-be."

Birdie glares at her. "Or else what?"

"Or else our friendship is over."

Birdie straightens. "You don't mean that," she says, although she's never seen Max more serious in her life.

"Damn right I do. I've held my tongue long enough, hoping you'd come to your senses on your own. It is way past time for you to rejoin the rest of the world."

Max grips Birdie by the arm and marches her over to the bathroom. "Get in the shower. And be sure to wash your hair. I'll pick out something for you to wear." Max shoves her into the bathroom and closes the door. "And hurry," she yells.

But Birdie takes her time in the shower, relishing the warm water massaging her aching muscles. As she towels off, she feels revitalized, more human than she has in the past fourteen days. *A proud grandmama-to-be.* How is she supposed to pretend to be that?

Max is right about one thing. It's not fair for Birdie to dump her business on her pregnant daughter.

Birdie forgoes drying her hair and putting on makeup. She slips on the yellow-and-pink floral sundress Max hands her and follows her best friend at a distance downstairs to the bakery. Hannah is opening her first gift when they arrive.

Hannah's friends and their mothers are extra generous in their gift-giving. They bestow expensive items on her—a stroller and car seat and bouncy seat. They feel sorry for her daughter. Poor Hannah, unmarried and pregnant. Poor Hannah, whose father embezzled money from his law firm and ran off with another woman.

Birdie is not one to get hung up on what other people think. But today, shame simmers within, alongside the anger and self-loathing.

Birdie forces a smile and graciously thanks the party guests for coming. She waits until everyone has gone except Max to inspect the gifts. She hasn't spoken face-to-face with her daughter in fourteen days, and she can't bring herself to meet Hannah's eyes. "You certainly got a lot of nice gifts. How will you get all this stuff to California?"

"Liza offered to drive out with me and fly home."

Her statement is a knife to the heart. "So, you're still moving to California?"

"Yes, Mom. Nothing's changed while you were . . . um, *sick*. I have a job waiting for me."

Max pulls Hannah in for a half-hug. "But you'll be here for a while after the baby comes, won't you?"

"About a month, give or take a week," Hannah says, smiling warmly at Max.

Birdie doesn't remember her daughter ever looking at her with the same affection as she's showing Max.

With Max's help, Hannah and Birdie move the gifts up to the living room, piling them neatly in a corner. When Max announces she's leaving, Hannah walks her to the stairs.

"Thank you for the shower, Max. Whether you admit it, I know you helped plan it."

Max cups Hannah's cheek. "You have very good friends on Palmetto Island."

After Max leaves, Hannah turns to face Birdie. "I've been working on a surprise for you. Wanna see it?"

Taken aback, Birdie places a hand on her chest. "For me? Sure. What is it?"

"I created a website for the bakery." Hannah motions for Birdie to follow her into her bedroom where an iMac computer is set up in front of the window.

"How did you get your old desk here?"

"Sadie's sons helped me. One of them has a truck."

"And the computer? That's new."

"I bought it with money I made from selling my photographs. It's hard to design websites on a laptop."

Hannah has been busy while Birdie was holed up in her room feeling sorry for herself.

Hannah sits down at the desk and, with Birdie peering over her shoulder, scrolls through the pages of the website. The visually appealing graphics stand out on clean web pages.

"Very nice, Hannah. I'm impressed. Can customers place orders online?"

Hannah cranes her neck as she looks back at Birdie. "The site has that capability, but we should wait until you have a process in place for filling orders before implementing it."

Excitement flutters in her tummy. "That makes sense. We'll need to think it through. I'd probably have to hire additional employees."

"By the way, I found a replacement for Jason. I think you'll like Amanda. She's a hard worker."

"I look forward to meeting her." Birdie reaches for Hannah's hand, giving it a squeeze. "I'm sorry you had to deal with so much in my absence."

"I didn't mind. But you're back now, though, right?"

"Right." Birdie smiles and drops Hannah's hand. When she turns away from the computer, her mouth falls open at the sight of Hannah's crib. "How'd that get here?"

Hannah walks over to the crib, running a hand across the railing. "I brought it over from the warehouse when I picked up my desk. Why didn't you ever mention it?"

"I never thought about it."

"Really? Surely you saw it when you were cleaning out the attic, preparing for the move. Are you afraid I'll get too comfortable and never leave Palmetto Island?"

"What on earth would make you say that? The last thing I want is for you to move to California."

Hannah rolls her eyes. "Yeah, right."

"I'm trying here, Hannah."

"And I never stopped *trying*, Mom. I've been *trying* to figure out how to make a life for this baby, and you've been *trying* to get me to give it away."

Hannah grabs the doorknob, opening the door a little wider, an invitation for Birdie to leave. "Look, Mom. I don't want to upset you. Please don't go hitting the bottle again. Let's just stay out of each other's way. As soon I get back on my feet after the baby comes, I'll leave town, and you'll never have to see me again."

TWELVE

Hannah thinks a lot about trust in the coming days. Even though she had a closer relationship with her father, her mother was the one who took care of her when she was sick and picked her up on time from school and her many extracurricular activities. Even when her mother had a few too many drinks at night, Birdie was always up early to feed Hannah a hearty breakfast before she left for school.

When, exactly, did she stop trusting her mom? The question plagues Hannah's thoughts. And the answer comes to her in a moment of clarity. When her father abandoned them. Hannah didn't lose faith in her mom. Her father is the one she no longer trusts.

Hannah studies Birdie as she works in the kitchen—her intense focus and serene expression as she rolls out pastries—and the way she interacts with customers. The patrons enjoy talking to her. How did Hannah not know her mother was so charming and witty? Because she doesn't know Birdie, the person, at all. She only knows Birdie, the mom. Birdie, the parent who provided services for her. Her father was the parent who provided the fun.

Hannah tries harder to get along with Birdie. And she senses Birdie trying harder, too. *The last thing I want is for you to move to California.* Is it possible Birdie really means it?

Hannah thinks often about her conversation with Liza. *I love being on the coast. Salt water runs through my veins.* Hannah feels the same way. The inlet is the one constant in her life she can rely on. She can count on the tides to rise and fall every twelve hours. For the wildlife to reproduce and feed their offspring. For the marsh to change colors with the seasons—from green to yellow to brown.

With Birdie back at work, Hannah gains time to focus her attention on web design. Redoing the florist website for Miss Allison is mundane work. But building a website from scratch to showcase Miss Jenny's library of romance novels offers real gratification. Miss Jenny is thrilled with the outcome and recommends Hannah's services to many of her author friends. And overnight, Hannah has more business than she can manage.

As July transitions into August, Hannah becomes increasingly more uncomfortable. She feels like she's carrying around a seven-pound watermelon. The baby presses on her bladder, and she has to pee every few minutes. Until now, she's gotten by with wearing her stretched-out yoga pants and gym shorts with T-shirts, but when those garments no longer fit, she rifles through Birdie's box of old maternity clothes for the least offensive garments.

On Wednesday of the first week of August, Max and Hannah take Birdie to Shaggy's to celebrate her birthday. They've no sooner been seated at a table on the deck when Max receives a call from her night desk clerk. "I have an emergency at the hotel," she explains when she hangs up. "I'll come back if I can, but don't wait for me."

Hannah suspects a setup. Max wanted Hannah and Birdie to have dinner together alone. The weather is pleasant and the food delicious as always. They talk about the pros and cons of adding e-commerce to the bakery website while they eat.

"Let's give it a shot," Birdie says. "Worst-case scenario, it ends up being too much for us to handle and we take it down."

"I'll look into it tomorrow," Hannah says.

The waiter clears their dinner plates and brings two slices of turtle pie. "Courtesy of Max," he says as he lights a candle in Birdie's pie. Other waitstaff gather around and sing "Happy Birthday" to a blushing Birdie.

Hannah catches her mom eyeing a glass of wine on a nearby table. "Is it hard not drinking?"

"You have no idea. But I hope you never have to find out." Birdie sets her fork down next to the half-eaten slice of pie. "I had so much time to think while I was hiding out in my room, but it wasn't until I came back to work that the fog lifted, and I was able to see things clearer. You asked me recently if your father was the reason I started drinking. For the longest time, I blamed my unhappiness and subsequent drinking problem on him. But the truth is, I have no one to blame but myself."

Hannah leans in, as close as the baby will allow. "You don't have to tell me all this, Mom. I know it must be hard to talk about."

Birdie shakes her head. "I need to say it. Make no mistake, Hannah, I willingly gave up nursing to be a stay-at-home mom for you. Those were the happiest years of my life, and I would do it all over again given the choice. But as you got older, you needed me less and less. My days lost their purpose, and I became lonely, and I started drinking. I should've taken responsibility for my own life instead of relying on you and your father to provide my happiness. I'm only human. I make mistakes. But I *am* trying."

Hannah nods. "I can see that."

Birdie's lips turn up in a soft smile. "And I can see you are too."

Hannah straightens in her chair. "I have my weekly appointment with Dr. Pendleton late tomorrow afternoon. If

Sadie and Amanda will close the bakery, maybe you can come with me."

Birdie doesn't hesitate. "I would absolutely love that."

The sound of her grandchild's heart beating takes Birdie's breath away. She heard this sound often as an ER nurse, but never coming from inside her daughter's womb. How could she have encouraged her daughter to have an abortion? To put her baby up for adoption?

"Strong heartbeat," Dr. Pendleton says and moves on to the pelvic examination. "The baby has dropped, you're fully effaced, and three centimeters dilated. You could go into labor at any time."

Hannah's olive eyes grow wide. "But I'm not due for another week."

Pendleton removes her surgical gloves. "And it may be another week before this baby's ready to come. But I highly doubt it."

After the appointment, mother and daughter walk in silence out to the car. "What're you thinking?" Birdie asks as she drives out of the parking lot.

"That I'm not ready for this."

Birdie glances over at her. "Few women are ever ready to become mothers for the first time."

"I'm emotionally ready. But I haven't finished preparing." Hannah shifts her gaze from the window to Birdie. "I've written all my thank-you notes, but I haven't gone through my shower gifts or washed any of the baby clothes. The baby book talks about nesting. But I haven't experienced that urge." Her expression is horror stricken. "Is there something wrong with me? Am I maternally flawed?"

Birdie pats Hannah's thigh. "Not at all. You're just unsettled, uncertain of where you'll be living."

Hannah furrows her brow. "You mean, because I don't have my own apartment?"

"Because you're moving to California." Birdie parks the car behind the bakery but leaves the engine and air conditioner running. She repositions her body toward Hannah. "Are you sure this move is what you really want?"

Hannah pauses for a long time before she answers. "Honestly, no. But I already accepted the job. They gave me a signing bonus."

"I have some money stashed away. I can—"

"No! That's not it. I haven't spent a dime of the bonus. I can give it back. Are *you* sure you want me to stay here?"

"More than anything. I owe you an apology, sweetheart. I was wrong in encouraging you to put the baby up for adoption. Won't you please consider staying on Palmetto Island?"

"I'm not sure, Mom. I have to think about it." Hannah gets out of the car and hurries inside.

Birdie throws the car in reverse and speeds down the alley to Ocean Avenue. She's trying so hard, but nothing she's doing is working. She's going to lose her daughter. She waits for traffic to clear to take a left toward the liquor store. *Don't do it, Birdie. Don't go down that path again. You will lose Hannah for sure.* Before she changes her mind, she makes a right instead. As she drives over the causeway to the beach, she rolls down her window, inhaling the salty air. She's made so many mistakes, been wrong about so many things, but she's going to survive. She heard her grandchild's heartbeat today. Hannah's flesh and blood. Birdie's flesh and blood. All is right with the world. If she has to move out to California to be near Hannah, so be it.

She makes a U-turn and drives back over the causeway, stopping in at the seafood market on her way home.

Hannah greets her at the top of the stairs. "Where'd you go?" she asks in an accusatory tone.

"To get some soft-shell crabs for our dinner." Birdie holds up the shopping bag as evidence.

"Yum. I'm going through the baby shower gifts. Wanna help?"

"Sure! Let me put these in the fridge, and I'll be right there."

Hannah and Birdie spend the evening getting Hannah's room ready for the baby. It's after nine o'clock before they work on dinner. Birdie sautés the soft-shells while Hannah chops up cabbage for coleslaw and butters chunks of warmed cornbread.

They take their dinner on trays up to the apartment and sit by the window watching lightning crack off in the distance as they eat. "Looks like a storm's coming," Hannah says.

"According to the weather report, it's supposed to storm all night." Birdie drags a crab claw through her puddle of tartar sauce and pops it in her mouth. "I have a confession to make. When I left here this afternoon, I was headed to the liquor store. But the thought of losing you for good made me go the other way. If you're determined to go to California, I'll sell the bakery and come with you. I want to help raise your baby. More than anything, I want to be a part of his or her life."

A smirk appears on Hannah's lips. "I made an impulse decision while you were gone. I hope you approve."

Birdie pinches off a bite of cornbread. "My days of judging you are over. Whatever you did, whether or not I approve, I'll support you."

"I called Jeff Brandon, my contact at the company in California. I told him I'm not taking the job."

Birdie's jaw falls open. "What'd he say?"

"He was very professional and understanding. I didn't tell

him about the baby, but I admitted our family has been through a recent crisis, meaning Dad's disappearance, and I felt like I needed to stay closer to home."

"That's wonderful news, honey. But are you sure?"

"I'm absolutely positive. I've been having doubts about this job all summer. And not just about the logistics of living in California. I think cyber security would bore me to tears. My web design business is booming. I really want to see where that takes me."

Tears fill Birdie's eyes. "You have no idea how happy you've just made me."

"I'm happy too, Mom. We still have some issues to work through, though. I can't have you drinking around the baby."

"I understand, sweetheart. I'll do my best."

"And that's good enough for me." Hannah sets her tray on the coffee table and rises slowly off the sofa. "I'm gonna get some more tea. Do you want some?"

Birdie smiles up at her daughter. "I'm fine. But thank you."

Hannah takes a step toward the stairs and doubles over with a hand pressed against her abdomen. "Oh, God. I think my water just broke."

Birdie looks down at the small puddle at Hannah's feet. "Let's get you to the hospital." She jumps up and carries their trays to the kitchenette.

"Mom!" Hannah shrieks. "I feel like I need to push."

"That's the baby bearing down on your cervix. You have hours before it's time to push."

Birdie grabs her purse and Hannah's small overnight bag, and they head off to the hospital. The storm is raging, and she's forced to drive slowly in order to see the road through the driving rain. Hannah's contractions are closer together, the pain intensifying with each one.

"Mom! It hurts so bad. Am I dying?"

"No, honey. You're having a baby. Hang in there. We're

almost at the hospital."

In the parking lot, Birdie finds a space close to the entrance and they hurry inside the emergency room. While filling out the paperwork, Hannah says, "I'm scared, Mom. Please don't leave me."

Birdie cups her daughter's cheek. "I'm not going anywhere."

As with most first babies, Hannah's labor is long, and Hannah pushes for what seems like hours before giving birth to a healthy baby boy.

Hannah's eyes glaze over. "A boy," she repeats as she falls back against the pillows. The nurse swaddles the baby and places the bundle in Hannah's arms. "Meet your son."

After Dr. Pendleton delivers the placenta, she says, "We'll give you a minute alone," and exists the room, taking the nurses with her.

Birdie pulls the blanket away from the baby's face to get a better look. "He's beautiful, Hannah. Does he have a name?"

With tears on her cheeks, Hannah says, "I'm going to name him Augustus. Gus for short."

This surprises Birdie. The name sounds so old-fashioned. "Augustus is a fine name, a strong and dignified name." *A family name,* she thinks but doesn't say out loud.

"Augustus is his father's middle name."

Birdie's heart skips a beat. "You mean, you know who the father is?"

"Duh, Mom. I'm not the kinda girl who sleeps around. We were in a relationship. We broke up after he cheated on me. He doesn't know about the baby, and I have no intention of telling him." Hannah kisses the top of the baby's bald head. "This baby is mine. Promise me, you won't tell anyone."

Birdie eases down to the edge of the bed. "I'll keep your secret, honey, but I urge you to reconsider. Whether it's five, ten, or fifteen years down the road, this decision will one day come back to haunt you."

ALSO BY ASHLEY FARLEY

Hope Springs Series

Dream Big, Stella!

Show Me the Way

Mistletoe and Wedding Bells

Stand Alone

Tangled in Ivy

Lies that Bind

Life on Loan

Only One Life

Home for Wounded Hearts

Nell and Lady

Sweet Tea Tuesdays

Saving Ben

Sweeney Sisters Series

Saturdays at Sweeney's

Tangle of Strings

Boots and Bedlam

Lowcountry Stranger

Her Sister's Shoes

Magnolia Series

Beyond the Garden

Magnolia Nights

Scottie's Adventures

Breaking the Story

Merry Mary

ACKNOWLEDGMENTS

I'm grateful to many people for helping make this novel possible. Foremost, to my editor, Patricia Peters, for her patience and advice and for making my work stronger without changing my voice. A great big heartfelt thank-you to my trusted beta readers —Alison Fauls, Kathy Sinclair, Anne Wolters, Laura Glenn, Kate Rock, Jan Klein, Lisa Hudson, and Lori Walton. And to my behind-the-scenes go-to girl, Kate Rock, for all the many things you do to manage my social media so effectively.

I am blessed to have many supportive people in my life who offer the encouragement I need to continue the pursuit of my writing career. I owe an enormous debt of gratitude to my advanced review team, the lovely ladies of Georgia's Porch, for their enthusiasm for and commitment to my work. To Leslie Rising at Levy's for being my local bookshop. Love and thanks to my family—my mother, Joanne; my husband, Ted; and the best children in the world, Cameron and Ned.

Most of all, I'm grateful to my wonderful readers for their love of women's fiction. I love hearing from you. Feel free to shoot me an email at ashleyhfarley@gmail.com or stop by my website at ashleyfarley.com for more information about my characters and upcoming releases. Don't forget to sign up for my newsletter. Your subscription will grant you exclusive content, sneak previews, and special giveaways.

ABOUT THE AUTHOR

Ashley Farley writes books about women for women. Her characters are mothers, daughters, sisters, and wives facing real-life issues. Her bestselling Sweeney Sisters series has touched the lives of many.

Ashley is a wife and mother of two young adult children. While she's lived in Richmond, Virginia for the past 21 years, a piece of her heart remains in the salty marshes of the South Carolina Lowcountry, where she still calls home. Through the eyes of her characters, she captures the moss-draped trees, delectable cuisine, and kindhearted folk with lazy drawls that make the area so unique.

Ashley loves to hear from her readers. Visit Ashley's Website @ashleyfarley.com

Get free exclusive content by signing up for her newsletter @ ashleyfarley.com/newsletter-signup/

facebook.com/ashleywfarley

twitter.com/AshleyWFarley

instagram.com/ashleyfarleyauthor

Made in United States
Orlando, FL
21 April 2022